SONG OF THE
SILENT SNOW

Other Works by Hubert Selby Jr.

Last Exit to Brooklyn
The Room
The Demon
Requiem for a Dream

SONG OF THE SILENT SNOW

Hubert Selby, Jr.

GROVE PRESS
New York

Published by Grove Press, Inc.
920 Broadway
New York, N.Y. 10010

Library of Congress Cataloging-in-Publication Data

Selby, Hubert.
     Song of the silent snow.

     Reprint. Originally published: London ; New York :
Marion Boyars, 1986.
     I. Title.
[PS3569.E547S6 1987]   813′.54   87-7388
ISBN 0-802-13008-9

Manufactured in the United States of America
First Edition 1987

10 9 8 7 6 5 4 3 2

To my wife Suzanne
who sang the song with me

Contents

Fat Phils Day

I used to get out of Sunday School about 10:30 or so and wake up some of the other guys and we/d wait on the corner for the crap game to start. We had one every Sunday no matter how cold or how lousy the weather was. And Fat Phil would be out by 8 with his shine box and get everyone goin ta church, from the 9 oclock Mass to the 11:30. He/d stand on the corner and look poor and neglected and he/d make out like crazy. If anybody asked him how old he was he/d knock off 3 years and say 10 and tell them he had to help support the family. He had some line and the churchgoers really ate it up. Anyway, after he finished shinin shoes he/d come down to 3rd Avenue and get in the game. Usually me and Fritz would play until we only had a dime left and save that for the movies, but sometimes we/d win a few bucks. But this Sunday Phil got on a hot roll and was cleanin everybody. Danny, a halfassed hustler from 43rd Street, usually came around and bet wrong, but he wasn't there today so the rest of us had to keep goin against the Greek. If Danny was there we could have jumped on Phils hot roll, but he wasnt. Anyway, everytime Phil threw the dice he/d throw a natural or if he got a point he/d hit it anyway. After about 7 or 8 passes he was taking all kinds of bets and winning: gagging his point, the hard way, over and under 7, anythin anybody wanted to lay and he won. We tried everythin to get him off the roll, jonahin against, then with, gaten the dice, but still he/d win. And everytime he threw another pass he/d roar and yell shootit, comeon ya bastads, fade me. Im hot. Comeon comeon, whos gonna fade me – halfabuck still open and somebodyd throw the money down, he/d roll the dice and hit another pass and roar and scoop up the money an we tried gaten the dice every other roll but he still won and everybody was goin broke and we started slappinim on the head and takin the polish from his shine box and he/d run after it and come back and throw the dice and hit another pass and roar that he was gonna take us all to the cleaners and Booby gaveim a shot in the arm and toleim if he didnt crap out he/d break his head and Phil still won but now he didnt laugh so loud and everytime he picked up the money we kickedim in the ass or rappedim off the head, but he couldnt lose. He hit 4 for a point and Sal madeim take an even money bet that he wouldnt do it the hard way and Phil almost cried but he put his money down and threw the dice and two twos came up and Sal toleim he/d break his shine box over his fat Greek head if he didnt crap out and he said hed pass the dice and Sal toleim he/d play until he crapped out or we/d killim and he picked up the dice and threw another natural and we were really punchinim now and he almost cried but still scrambled after the money and we kicked his ass, ya fat sonofabitch. Comeon fellas, leave me alone – rap – comeon. Gimme my brush – rap – please – another pass – stopit guys. Comeon willya? And he covered his head waiting for us to fade him and he hit a point and when he picked up the dice we rapped him and kicked him and he stopped pleadin with us and started pleadin with the dice come 7, please a 7 and he threwim again and again and it finally came up 4-3 and he jumped up and yelled SEVEN! There ya are, a 7. I lose, I lose. A 7 – 7! and he grabbed his shine box and ran like hell.

Hi Champ

He found a place at the middle of the bar and ordered a drink, smiling at the bartender. The bar wasnt too crowded, yet, but he knew that soon people from nearby offices would be coming in, and then the dinner crowd, and others for pre-theater cocktails. The bartender brought his drink and smiled, How are you tonight?

O fine. Just fine. Harry picked up his drink and looked around to see if he was there yet, but he did not see him anywhere. But that was to be expected, he never got here this early. He tasted his drink, then put it down. He wasnt too interested in drinking, though he did not mind a few once in a while. Actually he had drunk more in this past week than he had at any time in his life. Maybe in his entire life . . . or at least in a year. But this was Friday and tomorrow night was his date with Rita so he had to talk to him tonight. It was now or never . . .

He really did not know what he was afraid of. It was just a simple request and he could either say yes or no. That was it. He couldnt understand why he was having such a hard time asking. Why he felt so embarrassed. He had been coming here to Jack Dempseys every night this week trying to ask him and somehow he just never got around to it. He would go home and think about it and realize how simple it was and make up his mind to just walk over to him, smile, and ask him, and that would be that. And all day at work he would continue to tell himself that there was nothing to it and look forward to the evening when he would ask him, but then as he stood at the bar, waiting, mentally rehearsing, something inside of him seemed to freeze and he could not walk from the bar to where Jack Dempsey stood greeting people. He knew his request was not unusual, that all he had to do was walk over to him and smile, Hi champ, my names Harry Lewis.

Hi Mr. Lewis. How are you this evening?

Great. Real great, champ.

Good.

I was wondering if you would do me a favor?

I can try. What is it?

Im going to be here tomorrow night, for dinner, with a particular young lady and I was wondering if you would call me by my first name, you know, make a good impression.

Of course – he was smiling at Harry – I/d be delighted to, Harry.

Theyd laugh and Harry would go back to the bar feeling elated and then on his way home he would play the tape of him and Rita walking in and Jack Dempsey putting his arm around Harrys shoulder and greeting him like a long lost brother. He was a little surprised that the tape had not worn itself out.

Every day and every night this week he played that tape, over and over, and still he was standing here waiting. But he could not wait any longer. His date was tomorrow night. He looked around ... still nowhere to be seen. He looked at his watch. Another fifteen minutes or so. Tonight what I/ll do is just go over to him as soon as he gets here. Not take any chances of him getting caught up in conversations .... Yeah, thats the best thing. He nodded his head and finished his drink and ordered another.

He was vaguely aware of bits of conversation around him as the bar started filling, but he directed his attention more and more at the door, smiling as people edged their way to the bar. The more crowded the bar became, and the more people slapped backs, laughed greetings and bought each other drinks, the more isolated Harry felt. I must be the only one here alone.

And there seemed to be more people than usual, many more people ... and more laughter, louder talk, more ... more ...

more energy. Something. He could feel it. It made him nervous and edgy. He looked around the bar as discreetly as possible and no one seemed to be looking at him directly, but he had to admit that it was only logical that they would be talking about him as he was there alone, obviously not part of the *in* crowd. Maybe they thought of him as some sort of interloper or Johnny come lately ... or just some kid who happened to pass by or – Harry suddenly felt hemmed in by the people around him. It was weird but he almost felt like running, well not literally *running*, but leaving. But he knew he couldnt. He had to see the champ, tonight! His body seemed to become more and more tense and he felt increasingly aware of what was going on in his head, and the combination confused him and forced him to inch away from the others in the bar, and then, when he saw Jack Dempsey walking toward the door, he felt propelled in his direction. Ah ... a, a Mr. Dempsey, could –

Hi. How are you? He stuck his hand out and smiled.

Harry shook his hand and his head bobbed up and down a few times. Ah okay, a fine ... a just fine. He tried to smile but his face kept creasing into a grin. A, how are you?

Top shape. Couldnt be better.

Harrys head continued bobbing as he fought his grin into a smile. I was wondering if I could ahh ... you know ... if I could ask – Harry could feel his face going through all sorts of pinched contortions and he fought desperately to stiffen himself so he would not fall flat on his face ...

Can I do something for you?

Harry almost screamed with relief as he nodded, then almost screamed in despair as he realized he could not stop his damn head from bobbing up and down. He finally grinned it into submission. Harry took a deep breath, Im going to be here tomorrow night for dinner with someone and I would appreciate it if –

Dempsey smiled reassuringly, You want to make an impression on a girl, eh?

Harry refused to allow his head to bob and grinned as little as possible. Yes.

No problem. Whats your name?

Harry. Harry Lewis. I really appreciate yo –

Always like to help someone out. He put a hand on Harrys shoulder, Anytime Mr. Lewis.

Harry could feel himself grinning up at him.

I've got to go. See you tomorrow night.

Harry watched him walk away and just allowed his head to bob . . .

Then he was outside. In the air. It felt good. O God it felt good. He wasnt grinning. He hoped. He could see clearly. Head must not be bobbing. Face feels strange . . . he chuckled. Must be relaxed. He was walking. Stopped. Looked around, Where am I???? O yeah. Okay. He slowed his pace. Plenty of time . . . plenty of time . . .

Saturdays always took care of themselves. No thinking and almost no planning was necessary. He simply did the things that could only be done on Saturday such as the cleaning, the laundry, shopping, and the odds and ends that pile up during the week. The laundromat was just around the corner and he went to one store while the clothes were washing, and another while they were drying, but waiting for the machines to be available took up most of the time. That was when he caught up on his magazine reading.

When he got back to the apartment he straightened it up a bit and puttered around, listened to a little music and watched an old horror film on TV. It was not until late in the afternoon that he started to think about his date with Rita. Soon it was time to get dressed and leave.

Rita smiled as she opened the door, Come on in. But dont go too far or youll be out the back door. At least you would if there was a back door. Rita chuckled and Harry laughed. I just have to put on my coat and I/ll be ready. I used to live in a larger place, with a roommate, but I decided I would rather have something like this and have privacy.

Harry helped her on with her coat. I feel the same way. I like to be free to do what I want when I want . . . and with who I want.

She went to the door, Be careful, Im going to open the door. She laughed.

They stood on the corner waiting for a cab. I thought we/d go to Jack Dempseys for dinner. I havent been there for a while and I suddenly had the urge to see if its still the same.

She smiled, Thats fine with me. I dont think Ive ever been there.

Its been quite a while since Ive been there, but I think youll like it.

Harry made a conscious effort to relax as they entered the restaurant. There was a party of six in front of them and though Jack Dempseys voice could be heard they could only get a glimpse of him. The Maitre'd came over and escorted the party to their table and suddenly Jack Dempsey was standing in front of Harry and Rita.

Jacks face brightened and beamed, Harry, Harry Lewis, how are you? Jack patted Harry on the back and shook his hand, How have you been?

Just fine, champ. Moving right along. You know.

Yeah. I know.

O Jack, I/d like you to meet my friend Rita.

Hi.

Pleased to meet you.

Youre looking great, champ.

You know me Harry. Jack called the Maitre'd, Henry, Mr. Lewis would like a quiet table out of the way.

Henry nodded, Of course. This way please.

See you, champ.

They sat and Harry opened his napkin and felt like opening his arms. He felt expanded and expansive.

Rita smiled, I didnt know you knew Jack Dempsey.

Well, we/re not exactly bosom buddies, but . . . you know.

I think thats terrific. Im really impressed.

Harry smiled and nodded in acceptance of the compliment. Hes really a very nice guy you know. I mean a regular guy.

I like the way he speaks. I guess I must have been expecting some sort of rough – she shrugged her shoulders – certainly not such a nice, gentle man.

Yeah, the movies have tended to stereotype certain –

Would you care for a drink before dinner?

Harry looked at the waiter for a second . . . Yes, I think so. I/ll have a dry martini, very dry. How about you?

Yes that will do fine.

When the martinis came Harry sipped his . . . Thats good. I dont like to taste the wine, or even smell it. He smiled. The dryer the better.

I dont think Ive ever noticed. She picked up her drink, Well heres to you, champ. They both chuckled.

Everything went smoothly. They enjoyed the food and each others conversation. There did not seem to be any embarrassing lulls in the conversation, or any lulls at all for that matter. They both contributed to the conversation and they went from one subject to another, listening, talking, both feeling relaxed in the others company.

When they left the resaurant Harry waved at Jack, So long, champ.

He smiled and waved back, Have a good night.

Well, what would you like to do now Rita?

Did you have anything special in mind?

Harry shook his head, No. Im loose and open.

Rita had an almost impish smile on her face. Well, theres a horror film festival at that theater on East 12th. I think theyre showing Frankenstein and the Bride of Frankenstein tonight.

Hey, no kidding. Thats terrific.

There was a sound of glee in Ritas voice, Would you like to go?

Love it. I always did like Elsa Lancaster.

They both laughed and held hands as they walked to the corner to get a cab.

The theater was filled with afficionados and there was a feeling of excitement. Harry and Rita settled into their seats, enjoying the movies, and each others company, sharing their enjoyment and thus increasing it.

When they left the theater they both automatically, and almost simultaneously, took a deep breath, almost sighing as they exhaled. They looked at each other and laughed.

Like to go around to the Cedar for a nightcap?

No, I dont think so, champ. Im not much for drinking. If you dont mind?

No, not at all.

Why dont we pick up a cheese cake, or something, and go up to my place and I/ll make a pot of coffee.

Sounds terrific. Im all for that.

Harry put his arm around Ritas shoulder as they walked leisurely down the street.

When Rita unlocked the door she told Harry to be careful, dont go too far, youll bump into a wall.

Harry chuckled, I can always go out the back door instead.

Youd better wait until they build a stairway.

And a door.

Rita laughed. In the meantime give me that and make yourself at home. She took the cake from him and went into the kitchen. When the coffee was brewed they sat around the table eating the cake and drinking coffee.

Hmmmmm, this is good coffee. Whats the secret. Mines terrible.

Simple. Never clean the pot.

Harry almost choked as he laughed with a mouthful of coffee, trying desperately not to spit it out.

Youre terrific, absolutely great for my ego. You laugh at all my bad jokes.

I didnt know they were jokes.

Her coffee cup was at her lips when she started laughing and she held it tightly with both hands as she lowered it to its saucer. Maybe we should declare a truce and wait until we/ve finished the coffee before making any more cracks.

Okay – Harry raised his right hand – scouts honor. But you know, its hard not to be a little silly with you.

O . . . Rita raised an eyebrow and smiled.

Now dont start. We just made a pact. What I mean is – he shrugged – that I feel so relaxed. You make me feel so . . . so . . . at home.

Rita smiled appreciatively. Thank you. Thats a very kind thing to say.

Well, youre a very nice person – They smiled at each other unselfconsciously, taking pleasure in each others smile, and their own – And your idea of going to the flicks was a stroke of genius.

Well, to tell you the truth I was scheming all day how I could get you to take me there.

They laughed.

Well it sure didnt take much talking.

Rita stopped smiling and frowned slightly. Im sure that when they made those movies they were just trying to make a movie and nothing else, but I cant help reading things into some of them, especially the Bride of Frankenstein.

Harry leaned back in his chair and stretched out his legs, Like how?

Well ... well like every time man interferes with nature he creates a monster.

Harry nodded, I know what you mean. One of the most touching parts in that flick, for me, is when John Carradine stumbles around saying, Friend, friend ...

She nodded, He didnt want much, did he? Just someone to share what he had with. Funny how simple it seems sometimes to be happy and yet how easily it all gets confused.

Harry nodded and smiled and watched the way her eyes sparkled when she spoke and got excited, the way her mouth opened wide when she laughed, how all of her seemed to be happy with each laugh and just about everything that happened.

They continued talking easily, chuckling, smiling, and laughing their way from one subject to another, sometimes taking time out from the amusements to discuss something serious, each one finding they had respect and interest in what the other was saying, feeling uninhibited and speaking honestly about what they believed, enjoying both the smiles and the frowns of the conversation. Then Rita glanced at her watch, Wow, look at the time. No wonder Im feeling tired.

Harry looked at his, Yeah, youre right. Nothing like enjoying yourself to make time fly.

Rita nodded, then smiled. Would you like to spend the night?

Harrys smile was wide and warm, Cant think of anything I would rather do. They got up. But you had better lead the way, I dont want to go out that back door.

They laughed.

Almost immediately after getting into bed Harry put his arms around Rita and held her close to him. His mind was incredibly and abnormally quiet and unquestioning. He was absorbed by her and how she felt in his arms . . . She felt like her smile. They made love and it was completely satisfying for both of them and when they finished they lay on their sides, arms around each other, smiling and kissing, glowing . . .

until
they drifted into the softness of sleep.

Harry was the first to awaken in the morning. He looked at Rita for many moments, then gently got out of the bed so as not to awaken her. He had showered and dressed and was in the kitchen heating the coffee by the time she awoke. Hi.

Hi. Want a cup of coffee?

Rita shook her head, Not right now. Think I/ll bathe first. Isnt that kind of strong? Wouldnt you rather have fresh coffee?

No. Puts hair on your chest. He smiled and looked at her and wanted to touch her and lean over and kiss her but for some reason the sunlight pouring into the kitchen made it impossible. He tried to push himself forward, but was immobile. Have a good sleep?

She burst into a smile, O wonderful – she suddenly yawned – how do you like that? Isnt that something – she laughed – but I did. And I feel terrific.

Good.

You like lox and bagels and that sort of Sunday breakfast tradition?

Sure.

Theres a good Jewish deli on the corner. You could get some while I bathe and I/ll make us some scrambled eggs with lox.

Great. I/ll be careful opening the door.

She chuckled and Harry watched her as she walked to the bathroom.

The deli was crowded and by the time Harry got back Rita was in the kitchen. Here you are. I got a Times too. I figured if we/re going to be traditional then we should be traditional. They chuckled and Harry settled himself at the table with a cup of coffee and the Times while Rita started making breakfast.

When they finished eating Harry leaned back and sighed, My God, that/ll stick with me all day.

She smiled at him, Im glad you liked it. Im afraid I cant coast on it. I have to have dinner with my folks. She glanced at her watch, As a matter of fact I have to leave soon.

Thats too bad . . . Well, I guess I had better get going then.

If you wait a few minutes we can walk to the subway together.

Fine. Harry smiled, Why dont you take the magazine section. Something to read on the train.

Harry had an arm around Rita as they walked along the street, their bodies moving smoothly together. When they got to the subway they stopped. I/ll leave you here. Think I/ll take a bus.

Rita smiled up at Harry. I had a wonderful time last night. It was the nicest night Ive spent in a long time. Her face was glowing.

Yeah, me too. I wish it was an old movie. We could play it again anytime we wanted to. Harry chuckled.

That would be nice. I always was a softie for happy endings. O, you didnt give me your number. She looked through her pocket book, I have nothing to write on.

Thats alright. I/ll give you a call tonight.

About nine.

Fine. O here, dont forget the paper. He handed her the magazine section.

Thanks.

He kissed her and she felt soft and vibrant and when he separated his lips from hers he felt like sighing. Have a nice visit.

I will. Bye.

Harry watched her go down the steps, then turned and started walking to the bus stop.

When he got home Harry stretched out in a chair and without consciously directing his thoughts he started reviewing the night, and the morning, and he felt excited all over again. She was as nice as she was beautiful, and the most exciting woman he had ever met. He experienced again how she felt next to him, the softness of her skin under his hands, the warmth that came from her body . . .

and the way she smiled all over from somewhere deep within her. And she was so much fun to sit and talk with. It was incredible . . . And he had not felt awkward, not for a minute. He had never had an experience like that before in his life. There was always a little awkwardness, a little stammering or forcing of conversations, but none of those first-date things had happened. The entire evening, and morning, seemed to simply flow along some natural, divinely appointed course. It almost seemed unreal. God what a night . . . What a woman . . . What a joy. Yeah, what a joy. If its like that the first night, what will it be like later???? Things usually get better after people get to know each other, but how could it get better? It didnt seem possible. Everything was so perfect he did not see how it could be improved. Well, we/ll see. Give her a call tonight and then see what happens . . . Harry suddenly chuckled aloud as he remembered the long nights in Jack Dempseys trying to get up the courage to ask him the favor. How could such a simple thing have been so difficult? It doesnt seem possible. Not now. And he was so great. Its absolutely incredible. The whole week just to ask one little favor. And the whole night could have been ruined just by that. Who knows what would have happened if I hadnt finally asked him???? Might have been just another date. She sure was impressed by that reception he gave me. Yeah . . . she was *really* impressed. That probably was responsible for the whole evening. Might have an entirely different opinion of me if I hadnt arranged that. If she didnt think I was a friend of Jack Dempseys she might not have even wanted me to call tonight. Might have spent the night here instead of with her . . . But I did tell her we werent really close friends. I didnt lay it on too heavy. Just a little poetic license. Its really no ...

Yeah ...
Maybe she isnt going to her parents. Maybe she just wanted to have me leave. That business about my phone number could be just a game. If she really wanted it why didnt she ask for it before? Why did she wait until we were at the subway? There was plenty of time before. And what did she mean about happy endings? Ending what? If she doesnt want to see me again why doesnt she just say so????

So I dont really know Jack Dempsey. Thats no reason to play games. She didnt have to go through the charade of visiting her parents just so I wouldnt be hanging around all day. I would have left ...

But the whole night wasnt really built on a lie ... not really. Its not a real lie. Not like telling someone youre going to visit your parents just to get rid of them. *Thats* a lie. And telling them you like them when you dont. *Thats* a lie. And asking them for your phone number when you dont really want it. *Thats* a lie. The whole evening ... night .... and morning ...

a lie.

Just some-
thing to torture the loneliness that tries to stay hidden in every heart ....

But maybe she will be there at ni – no ... no. She wont ... Maybe ... Maybe she will ...

But whats the point? It wont make any diff-
erence. You know what it will be like. The embarrassment ... Why bother? There/ll just be another story ... another lie. Theres no point in calling. Its always the same ...

Its all over.

Double Feature

There was no tangible reason for feeling so great (unless you believe in astrology, but he didnt and wasnt aware of the positions of the constellations or the fullness of the moon) nor was it entirely due to it being Friday with two workless days ahead and 3 leisurely nights . . . though this, along with the warm weather of early summer, were partially responsible; but he wasnt attempting to define the reasons for this feeling. It was just there. That was enough. You dont plan it, you just enjoy it; relax and float along with it and laugh. Yeah, thats the secret, and as long as you control it youve got it made, but try to drag it by the arm and you/ll kill it . . .

No, he/d play it cool. Just go up to the Avenue and meet Chubby and maybe go to a show and then CHARLIES and listen to the group blow – have a few beers and . . .who knows? When you feel like this you dont have to go around looking for kicks.

He walked up 69th Street, smiling, to 4th Avenue and met Chubby in front of the pool room. Whatta ya say Chub, poking his arm and dancing on his toes, sparring. Whats with you Harry, been eatin happy pills? laughing and waving his left in Harrys face. Yeah. Anybody inside? No. A couple of the guys are in Phils talking about the game this afternoon. I bet Phils havin a ball. The Giants really clobbered the Dodgers today. A ball? Hes been roarin since the game ended. Yeah, I bet.

They laughed and Chubby took out a packet of cigarettes, put one in his mouth and held the match until Harry had gotten one out of his pack and lighted it. Whatta ya feel like doin tonight, Chub? I dont know. Kinda early to do anything now. Feel like taking in a show? I dont know. Whats playin? Theres a musical at the Bay Ridge. I saw the comin attractions last week. It looked pretty good. O yeah, a couple of the guys saw it and said it was great. Jimmy went ape in one scene. A redhead does a real wild dance. Sounds good. How about takin it in? O.K.

They left the avenue and walked down 69th Street, crossing to the shady side, to 3rd Avenue. Whos going to be at CHARLIES tonight? Im not sure. I met Mitch, the bass player, a little while ago and he said Buck Clayton might sit in tonight. No kiddin? Should be a good session then. Should be. Hes usually pretty cool. He said that kid who blew trombone last week might be there too. Great. He lets it get away from him sometimes, like hes trying to find somethin, but when he doesnt go too far out hes good. He should be real great someday. Remember that solo he took on A Small Hotel? Yeah. Man! He did some fine stuff on that. Never went crazy but blew it cool, real cool. He went way out on How High the Moon though. Yeah, he lost control of his horn on that one; Willie was poundin out the chords like crazy tryin to help him back. Hes good though. I hope he shows up tonight. I/d like to dig him and Clayton together. I guess he will. He probably gets kicks from playing with good boys like that. Yeah, I guess he does.

They turned left on 3rd Avenue and walked toward the movie. A block away Chubby suggested they stop in for a beer first. They went in to the bar on the corner, had 2 beers and a bag of peanuts, then left and continued toward the movie. A few minutes later Harry grabbed Chubby by the arm and suggested they bring a little something to drink with them. You know, just a pint of wine. For kicks. Chubby smiled, shrugged his shoulders. Why not?

They were both laughing as they bought the wine and a package of paper cups. We have to play it cool man. We dont want to look like winos. Chubby put the bottle in his hip pocket and walked in front of Harry so he could make sure it was hidden by his jacket.

The nearer they got to the box office the weirder going to the movies with a bottle of wine seemed. Even a little exciting. They tried to stiffen their faces in a natural expression and Chubby stood to one side as Harry bought the tickets, then walked behind him through the lobby, looking away as the man took their tickets. They climbed the stairs to the balcony two at a time before relaxing; then started looking for seats.

They found two empty seats on the aisle in the last row and sat quietly for a few moments. Then Harry told Chubby to open the package of cups. He started ripping the cellophane off slowly, the ripping sounding louder and louder. He stopped for a second, then ripped the remaining cellophane off at once and sat back and waited a moment before handing the bottle to Harry. He took the bottle from Chubby and immediately bent behind the seat in front as Chubby looked around, both of them giggling. Harry finally opened the bottle and Chubby passed two cups to him and he filled them, recapped the bottle and put it under the seat, then sat up. They forced their shoulders down, looked at the screen and sipped their drinks.

Most of the people in the audience were laughing and commenting to each other, but Harry and Chubby laughed as quietly as possible, keeping their comments to a whisper. When their cups were empty Harry ducked behind the seat again, taking fewer precautions, and refilled them. When he filled the cups for the third time the only precaution he took was not to spill any wine. They sat holding their cups loosely, resting them on the seat between their legs; lifting them while still watching the screen and drinking; leaning over toward each other to whisper a comment as a seminaked woman walked across the wide panoramic screen . . . and laughing. Finishing their 3rd cup they were relaxed and laughing as loudly as the others, but with less provocation, occasionally laughing while drinking, wine spluttering and dribbling down their chins. The woman continued walking and they sat choking, coughing, trying not to make too much noise and not to spill too much wine.

When Harry poured the last of the wine he put the bottle back with a clink and he and Chubby toasted each other and sipped slowly. When their cups were empty they dropped them to the floor and sat for a few minutes smoking, watching the movie and giggling. Then Chubby said he was getting thirsty. Yeah, me too. How about another bottle? Why not. Think theyll letya back in? Sure. I/ll tellem I want somethin in my car. Hey, how about gettin somethin ta nibble on? You know some popcorn or chips. Maybe youd like some ordurves already.

Harry started to laugh, then half closed his eyes after Chubby left and stared at the beam of light from the projector, watching the vague smoke drift toward it and then brighten, whirl and float through the ray . . . drifting deeper into his mood. He wasnt drunk, though he was a little lightheaded, as was Chubby, from drinking the wine rapidly in the warm theater, but he had a fine glow and was relaxed enough not to think or be concerned with just how relaxed he was. He was going to laugh and have one hellofagoodtime. There was no danger of killing the mood either by losing it or dragging it. He just drifted between the light, the smoke, the screen, one of the girls at work, CHARLIES, Clayton and the trombonist . . . but mainly sinking further and further into his contentment, his mind almost empty (forcing a silly grin of introspection), knowing this was going to be a good night, a good weekend. Not crazy wild. Just a lot of laughs . . .

Harry drifted, oblivious of place or time . . . Then Chubby appeared, sat down and took 2 bottles from his pockets and handed them to him. Thought I/d get an extra one. You know, just in case.

Harry laughed and took the bottles, put one under the seat, opened the other and filled a cup. While he was pouring Chubby took a full loaf hero sandwich from under his jacket. Harry didnt notice it, being too busy opening the bottle and pouring the wine, so it was just a blur seen from the side of his eye. When he turned to give Chubby his drink, Chubby was holding the sandwich horizontally, nibbling at the liverwurst hanging over the sides, humming *claire de lune* and waving his fingers like a harmonica player. The people around them were nudging each other and laughing, some tapping those in front of them and pointing to Chubby as he played the hero sandwich, Harry staring at him, holding a cup of wine. The laughter and craning of necks increased until almost that entire section of the balcony was ignoring the screen and watching the playing of the sandwich. Chubby turned to Harry and rolled his eyes and fluttered his lids, still fanning the sandwich and moving his shoulders to the music. Harry, his hand holding the cup of wine still extended toward Chubby, stared, chuckled, then laughed, the wine spilling over his hand and dripping on Chubbys pants, his hand slowly falling and the cup tilting until the wine poured out in a steady stream and splashed on their feet, their laughter growing louder, people turning in their seats, looking and laughing as Harry laughed and Chubby laughed, still playing the hero sandwich (his laughter, muffled by the sandwich, sounding weird), slowly bending over, sinking further down and almost about to double into a ball and roll down the stairs with a steady thump bump, thump bump, still laughing and playing the hero sandwich, when Harry dropped the cup, plop, fell on Chubbys shoulder and put his arms around him forcing the sandwich from his mouth, burying his face in Chubbys jacket.

They remained embraced until their laughter stopped, not from determination but exhaustion, then parted and sat back in their seats with a series of soft sighs. Slowly the attention of the others returned to the screen and the two sat, silent (except for an occasional involuntary snort), wanting and not wanting to look at each other, sitting slightly angled from each other (the sandwich resting on Chubbys lap), covering their faces with their hands . . .

Harry breathed deeply and without looking at Chubby told him to put that damn thing away. Chubby mumbled something, put the sandwich up his sleeve, said, Its o.k. now, and they turned slowly in their seats until they were once more facing the screen. Harry reached under the seat for the bottle and filled 2 cups, handed one to Chubby. They spoke to each other only after emptying their cups and refilling them. The hollowness created by their laughter was filled by the wine and as the warmth of relaxation increased they leaned towards each other and once more were whispering comments and laughing.

They drank more rapidly (the bottle being replaced with a clink), their heads barely apart, their elbows on the arm rest between their seats, lifting their drinking arms and tilting their heads back . . . each a reflection of the other. And, as they drank, their whispering, giggling and laughter grew louder, yet still not boisterous or annoying.

From making comments upon the action on the screen they progressed to prediction and then to direction; urging the girl-shy male star to kiss her, she wont bite . . . tittering, laughing, reaching for the bottle (clink) watching the wine being poured into the cup (plop, plop, plop), putting the bottle back (clink) – whatzamatta with that guy, is he nutsor somethin? If I had a broad like that runnin afta me I/d – swaying, wine sloshing in the cups; laughing, swallowing, bubbling, choking, wine splashing on their noses, dribbling down their chins, dark spots blotted by pants and shirts – reaching (clink), only a few drops left, watching the last drop plop into the cup, still one left (clink); two empties; good show, eh Chubb? Cups refilled (getting soft and soggy, dented, dont squeeze too tight, please dont squeeza the banana – held by the bottom in the palm of the hand); wheres the otha ones – all gone – no more haha – no (clink) more (bottle resting on his lap) – come fill me with the old familiar juice – HUH HUH – she slinks, semidressed, toward him, hair over the side of her face, hips liquid, rubs his cheeks then pushes her hands thru his hair, down his neck and back, sways in front of him, all virtues and charms (almost all) displayed, the voice throaty, begging . . . he asks her what she wants – *OOOOO whattza matta? ya crazy? HAHAHA* – He/d betta go ta Denmark – HUH HUH (cups squashed and dropped to the floor, the bottle passed back and forth), drinking in large gulps, small drops trickling down their chins and adams apples – she forces him back onto a couch, bends over him, gives him the look and kisses him . . . he kicks and waves his arms – I toldja they was all fruits in Hollywood – the struggling stopped, soft music – dont fight it, enjoy it HAHAHA – holding the bottle up, not much left, get somemore – OOOO please dont squeeza the banana; only a drink left; save me some, a gulp, ahhh . . . here . . .

rubbing his mouth with the back of his hand, empty bottle passed back (clink) – no more; all gone, three dead soldiers – HUH-HUHHUH –hey daddy, I wanna ice cream. Shaddup an drink ya beer. HEHEHE, that guys nuts – HUHHUHHUH, I cant HAHAHA – whatz he HEHEHEHE – the screen wavering and blurred ... images tumbling about ...HAHEHHUHHOHO-HEHHUHHHO ...

Please be quiet, sir. Youre disturbing the others. The usher finished his prescribed speech and duty and was turning to walk away when Chubby suddenly jumped up, whipped out his hero sandwich and started fencing with him, Un Guard!!!! He brandished the sandwich in front of the ushers face, parried thrusts, stepped aside as a lunging sword just missed his chest; parried again and with perfect execution and grace watched another thrust pass, then stooping low, left knee bent and right leg extended behind, he parried the last lunge and thrust home, TOUCHE!!!! piercing the usher, mortally, a little to the left of his second brass button. Chubby watched him slump to the floor, proud of his victory, yet with some regret at having killed so noble an adversary ... The sandwich bent slightly with the thrust and a piece of liverwurst fell on the ushers shoe. He stared at it for a moment (all he had intended to do was deliver his speech and leave and now he was standing in front of a drunk waving a hero sandwich and there was liverwurst on his shoe) until his head was forced up by the tip of Chubbys sword. Harry stood up and tried to speak in a high falsetto, but phlegm stuck in his throat causing his words to sound gargled, My HERGGO! Then he roared, leaned on Chubbys shoulder; Chubby roared, the sandwich hanging from his hand, the liverwurst dropping to the rug. Harry tripped over the bottles as he pushed Chubby out into the aisle, and they bounced clinkingly down the steps.

Harrys eyes were tearing and he bounced off the banister as he went down the stairs, Chubby behind him. They reached the first landing and turned to continue, half bent with laughter, stumbling, falling ... Chubby raised himself to his knees, holding his stomach, whining hysterically, saliva dribbling from his mouth – Harry felt sand under his nails, pulled himself up, heard a thump and continued stumbling down the staircase; banged through the doors (turning to look for Chubby expecting to see him roll down the stairs, ass and head, ass and head, ass and head, then careened out to the street. His momentum carried him to the corner where he leaned against the fender of a car, laughing . . . just laughing . . . not trying to stop or continue, not wondering where Chubby was; not thinking about the fencing scene or CHARLIES and the group or how he felt; not conscious of the saliva dripping down his chin; not even thinking of having another drink . . . just laughing . . . .

Then there were shadows, voices . . . then people. Thats the other one. O.K. buddy, comeon. A policeman grabbed his arm and they followed the usher and the manager back into the theater, hurried through the lobby and into the managers office. Chubby was sitting on a stool in the corner, another policeman in front of him, smoking and still smiling. Youre sure it was these two? O yes sir. Theyre the ones. Im sure. I dont know which one turned over the cigarette urn, but Im absolutely certain theyre the ones. You see I heard a dis – O.K., O.K. Thanks. You can go now.

The usher backed out of the office and the cop walked between Chubby and Harry, rubbed the knuckles of his right hand with the palm of his left and asked what-in-the-hell they thought this was, a gymnasium or something? Annoyed at being called and at Chubby's stupid grin (appearing insolent to him), but wanting to make an impression on the manager, knowing he never forgot a favor. He stepped in front of Chubby and slapped the cigarette from his mouth. His aim wasn't perfect and in knocking it out he burned his hand. He grunted, held his hand for a second and when he looked back, Chubby had the same stupid grin on his face. He grabbed him by the lapels of his jacket, slammed his head against the wall, slapped him a half dozen times, then shoved him into the chair.

Harry watched, not unseeingly, but uncomprehendingly, still incapable of forcing his mind to work. Somewhere there was a vague remembrance of a sound, but the only thing definite was laughter, thats all, laughter. He was leaning against the chair, laughing. That wasn't a memory. That must be what hes doing now, and all this is something else. What was wrong? That was Chubby. He recognized him. Hes still laughing; and it looks like wine trickling down his chin. Theres nothing wrong. We/re both laughing ... He started to take a step toward Chubby, but the other cop poked him, hard, in the stomach with his nightstick. Go ahead you sonofabitch. Start something. Just start something, tough guy.

Harry instinctively clutched his stomach, confused and still unable to understand what had and was happening. The cop turned back to Chubby and told him to give them his identification. Chubby handed him his wallet and the cop slapped him on the chest with it and told him he wanted his identification, not his wallet. Who do you think youre tryin to buy off? He grabbed the draft card from Chubbys hand. 19. Another one of those punks who thinks hes a big brave man because he has a draft card. Cant you think of anything better to do than sit in a movie drinking cheap wine and damaging property? The cop growled in the accustomed manner, no longer deliberate, but habitual, and stood in front of Chubby glaring at him as he did everyone else in the same position, expecting the face to be lowered and some sort of apology murmured and then he would yell for him to speak up, and when it had been repeated he would curse him, tell him hes lucky that hes not going to lock him up and then tell him ta get the hell home ... yet hoping, looking at the still smirking face, that he would give him some sort of wisecrack and afford him an excuse to slap his face again. Chubbys first attempt at speech was incoherent and slobbering. What? It washnt sheep. He didnt take time to enjoy the fulfillment of his wish, but swung immediately, knocking Chubby over the chair and to the floor. Chubby gradually sat up, his head hanging and rolling. The cop turned to Harry and asked him how old he was. Perhaps Harry didnt understand the question, or perhaps it just got jumbled in his mind. He didnt know (nor would he remember later), but for some reason (if there was a reason) he said, 76 (still a hint of laughter that needed only to hear someone else laughing or for Chubby to turn and smile to revive it, and then theyd be back outside [I dont think we/re there now] and could start over again, go to CHARLIES) he heard the slap, then another. Still nothing, but vaguely aware that now the laughter was gone, yet still not understanding. He thought he remembered a sound. Or was that imagined?

What do ya want us to do withem, Mark? The manager, upset at the slapping, looking at them on the floor, thinking of the reports that would have to be made, the explanations and reassurances given, if they were arrested ... Nothing, Jim. They didnt break the urn. No real damage done. Just kick them out and forget about it.

They were quickly jerked to their feet, taken out to the street and walked to the corner. They told Chubby to go up to 4th Avenue and Harry down to Ridge Boulevard. And if you give anybody any more trouble we/ll split your skulls open.

Harry turned when he reached Ridge Boulevard and staggered over to the school steps and sat down. He rested his head on his hands then noticed the small smear of blood on his palm. He couldnt taste it, but it must be real. But it didnt make any sort of sense. There wasnt any fight. Just laughing. We werent even drunk ... How? There wasnt even a beginning to go back to. I dont even know what time it is ...

He rubbed his face, the back of his neck, and looked at the tree a few feet in front of him and tried to find the sky. The red and amber traffic lights on the corner were blinking.

He fumbled through his pockets looking for a cigarette but couldnt find any. O shit! SHIT!!

He stared at the sidewalk for a moment, then slowly stood up, holding on to the fence, and started walking home ...

Fortune Cookie

Harry sat in a rear booth of the Chinese restaurant, alone and worried, toying with his chicken egg drop soup, occasionally eating a spoonful. The boss had not said anything to him directly, but he knew his time was coming . . . soon. He had not given Harry an ultimatum, but the looks and remarks – more than that, the feeling Harry got when he was around him, and was starting to get when he stepped into the office, and even over the phone, forced Harry to accept the fact that his time was coming. And he did not mean a feeling of anxiety. Harry knew what that felt like. He should, he had been living with it all his life and lately it had been getting worse by the day . . . day? Krist, it was getting worse by the hour and right now by the minute. It was more than anxiety, it was a realization.

A salesman sells. It is that simple. A salesman sells and when he doesnt he is not a salesman and who needs a salesman who is not selling. Firms do not carry non-selling salesmen for long. Actually he was lucky they carried him this long, even giving him his draw. But last week was his last draw and today could be his last chance. No sale today and . . . he stared at the soup for a minute, then pushed it away from him, the waiter quickly picking it up and replacing it with a dish of food. Harry moved his mouth into a quick smile then took a deep breath and started mixing the soy sauce into his chow mein.

He had to make that sale today. He had no choice. It was do or die . . . the knot in his stomach quickly started gnawing its way up to his throat and Harry took a deep breath and tried to relax, at least enough to eat. He ate some food and tried a little positive thinking. After all, he can do it. He can make this sale. He/ll just go in there, smile and relax, and let the product, and the customer, do the selling. Right! Thats all there is – but Ive been doing that for months and still no order. The chow mein looked heavy and soggy. But I lit another candle this morning and prayed and made the stations of the cross and I cant fail with all – but Ive been doing that for months too. He took another deep breath and tried to relax . . . then took a few mouthfuls of food. Cant get all caught up in superstition – not that praying is superstition, but I mean all that business about a lucky tie or suit . . . have to forget all about that . . . Yeah, even if I had a lucky tie or suit. Pretty soon I might not have a suit or tie – this is ridiculous. This suit and tie are just as lucky as any I have. He shrugged, Ive lost as many sales with them as with any other suit and tie . . . he chuckled inwardly and even smiled and turned his attention to the food for a while, the noodles seeming to be a little crispier. The knot of anxiety started growing and travelling again and he suddenly thought of his shoes, maybe these are my lucky shoes, and he started his silent chuckling again and kept the anxiety enough in control to finish most of his chow mein.

The waiter quickly cleared away the plates and brought a fortune cookie and the check. Harry played with the cookie for a few minutes, tapping it on the table, then eventually, almost absentmindedly, he broke it open and tugged the fortune out and glanced at it, the words not getting through his preoccupation at first, but a glimmer of something registered and he looked carefully at the fortune: Take courage, today is your day for success. He nodded his head, Yeah . . . sure. Then he stopped frowning and read it again and straightened, Why not? Why shouldnt it be my day? It has to be somebodys day and Ive had enough losers. Yeah . . . thats right, Ive had enough losers This *can* be my day as well as anyone elses . . . . Thats right . . . absolutely right. They need our material and they may just as well buy it from us as anyone else. We/re just as good as anyone and better than most. And we can deliver on time. Thats the big thing in this industry, guaranteed delivery as well as guaranteed quality. And we have it . . . all! Hed be doing himself and his firm a favor to place the order with us. Youre damn right! Harry nodded his head emphatically and reached in his pocket for his money, then stopped and reached instead for his credit cards, the ones he had been afraid to use for many months, and dropped one on the tray with the check and sat back, relaxed, exhilarated. He smiled broadly as he added a generous tip, then signed the slip with a slight flourish. He pocketed his card and stepped briskly from the restaurant.

His appointment with Mr. Dasher went smoothly and was successful beyond all expectations. Harry seemed to speak at exactly the right time and say exactly the right thing and was quiet at exactly the right time in the right way, listening intently and exuding an aura of relaxation and confidence. His whole attitude was one of having already made the sale and he was here to simply help Mr. Dasher in whatever way he could. At the end of their meeting Mr. Dasher was as happy as Harry and their final handshake and words were extremely cordial. Harry knew he had a lifetime customer.

Harry of course was elated as he headed back to the office with the signed order, so happy over making the sale he did not stop to figure out what his commission would be. When the thought did enter his mind he quickly shrugged it off knowing he would probably still be behind on his advances anyway. And he did not want to ruin the way he felt by thinking about the state of his finances. He had made a sale, a big sale. That was the important thing. He had broken his losing streak. He was a winner and for that he was grateful.

As soon as he gave the order to the proper people in the office he called his boss and told him. At first Mr. Wells sounded surprised, but that quickly changed to a tone of delight, Thats wonderful, Harry. Congratulations. I knew you could do it. Harry beamed and leaned back in his chair, nodding his head and thanking Mr. Wells for the compliments. He hung up and just sat for a few minutes allowing that good feeling to flow through him . . . then called his wife and told her the good news.

Harry sat quietly for a few more minutes, then looked at his watch, and started calling and making appointments, having no trouble getting appointments with the people and before he stopped his calendar was filled for the next couple of weeks.

Harry lit a candle the following morning, not wanting to break any part of the routine that led to the previous days success, but his attitude was different. He did not kneel and beg like a condemned man going through a ritual for the sake of propriety, knowing all along that it was useless and he would be led to the gallows anyway, but rather like a friend bringing a feeling of gratitude for the gift he knew he would be receiving.

Naturally Harry had lunch in the same restaurant. He was even going to order chicken egg drop soup and chow mein, but thought it safe to deviate slightly and have won ton soup and sub gum chow mein. The big difference today was again his attitude. He sat at a small table in the middle of the restaurant, smiling, and ate the food with deep enjoyment and relish.

When the plates were cleared away and the waiter brought his fortune cookie he leaned back in the chair, one arm over the back of the chair, nonchalantly toying with the fortune cookie and feeling a warm glow inside. He picked the cookie up and smiled as he rolled it around in his hand, tapped it on the plate, spun it around playing spin the fortune cookie and eventually leaned over and snapped it in half and extricated the fortune: Today is a day to assert yourself. He pulled his shoulders back, yeah, thats right. His back was straight as he walked from the restaurant, and self-confidence exuded from him.

He had scheduled two appointments for the afternoon and both went smoothly and ended in large orders just as he knew they would. He had the right combination now and had the world by the tail. He could not lose. That he knew. He could not lose. He was a winner.

The following day he started to get a slight premonition, a tremor, when he realized he would have to change his routine, but was steadfast in his refusal to allow it to shake his confidence. He had made a lunch appointment with one of his prospective clients who was across town and so there was no way they could have lunch in the Chinese restaurant next door. So Harry checked the yellow pages for Chinese Restaurants in the vicinity of the customers office and found one listed only a block and half away. When he suggested going there for lunch the other man agreed quite readily.

Harrys relaxed attitude helped relax his customer and they had a very enjoyable lunch. Harry did not toy with his fortune cookie, but ignored it as long as possible as they continued their discussion, then casually cracked it open and smiled as he read his fortune: Success comes to the successful man. Harry nodded inwardly, thats right, success breeds success and Im for inbreeding. The other man did not bother with his fortune cookie, so when they got up to leave Harry surreptitiously picked it up and put it in his pocket. Just might come in handy.

When Harry left the mans office 45 minutes later he had another large order. He called it in to his office then walked around for a short time until it was time to go to his next appointment. This one too went exactly as Harry knew it would – the other fortune cookie said it would – so that made two orders so far. Harry knew that sooner or later he would leave an office without a signed order, that was inevitable, but for now he was riding a hot streak and was going to give it all he had.

He also knew that the fortune cookies did not really have anything to do with the sales, but he was not going to take any chances and so he continued with the candles in the morning and the Chinese restaurant in the afternoon. And business was good. It was great! As a matter of fact his sales were mounting so rapidly that it looked like he would be a shoe in for the salesman of the year award. And as the sales mounted so did his commissions and it was obvious that he would have to start looking for some sort of tax shelter. He smiled and grinned when he thought about it, not exactly a bad position to be in.

Things continued going almost perfectly for several months. Even the people who did not give him an order were very favorably impressed, telling him they would keep him in mind if their situation ever changed. But eventually the inevitable fly came into the ointment and Harry had to find a way to get rid of the fly without throwing out the ointment. He became a victim of the Chinese restaurant syndrome.

The first time it struck he ended up being late for an appointment but fortunately no harm was done and he survived the attack and got an order. At first, as he sat on the commode doubled up with cramps and sweat pouring from his pores, he knew he would have to stop going to the Chinese restaurant every afternoon. Then, after he returned with the order and relaxed in his office, he realized that he was being hasty. Its not that he was being superstitious you understand, but it just did not make sense to change a routine that was working so well.

The following day convinced him. And though he knew that his sales did not depend upon his eating in a Chinese restaurant every day, he still tried to find some way of continuing to do so without getting sick. Or more specifically, to get the fortune cookie he needed – no, no, he didnt really need it, but . . . well, what the hell, everybody has some sort of good luck charm. Certainly no different than a rabbits foot. He shrugged inwardly, what the hell.

The next day he went to a small Chinese food take-out store and took the fortune cookie out of the bag and dropped the rest in the first litter can, then went to lunch. He glowed with pride at his ingenuity and the ease with which he had solved the problem. Each day he went to the take-out stand and ordered a few items and threw them away after taking out the fortune cookie.

One day he noticed a couple of girls from his office at the stand and continued walking, then came back ten minutes later, looking around carefully to make sure no one else from his office was there. Now when he left the office for lunch he glanced over his shoulder to be certain no one who knew him was in the vicinity, carefully looking around again before dropping the bag of food in a litter can as nonchalantly as possible, studying the sky and whistling as he hurried away.

Soon the pressure of this routine started to create anxieties so he would eat lunch in the area first, then go to a take-out stand some distance from the office to get his fortune cookie.

After much testing, and some trepidation, he found he could safely eat in a Chinese restaurant every fourth day without fear of an attack. And so he sampled the Chinese food from one end of town to the other. He was in Chinatown one day when he made a happy and astounding discovery: a store that sold fortune cookies by the bag. Now he truly had nothing to worry about.

He kept a bag of cookies in his desk drawer and rationed them out to himself, one at a time. But then it started becoming a little difficult to understand some of the fortunes. Well, it wasnt that they were hard to understand exactly, it was just that they were ambiguous or simply did not apply to the immediate situation. So Harry was forced to open another ... and another, until he found one that was pertinent to the day before going out on his appointments. Soon he had to buy bags by the dozen, wanting to be certain he did not run out, and when he left the office he was covered with cookie crumbs, the old anxiety giving him a slight twinge from time to time.

One morning Harry was studying reports and getting together information to present to a prospective customer. This was an international corporation and if Harry could close this particular deal it would be the largest in his firms history and would open undreamed of vistas for the firm and for Harry. Among other things it would mean an appointment to the Corporate Staff.

He had been working on it for six months, putting in endless hours and tremendous energy and creative imagination, and the final appointment, the yes or no appointment, was for tomorrow afternoon. He had everything together and was starting to review it again when he received a phone call advising him that his appointment for the following day would have to be cancelled, Mr. Ralston had to leave the country unexpectedly, and could Harry make the appointment for this afternoon at two, Mr. Ralston having no idea when he might be otherwise available.

Harry quickly agreed and automatically reached into his drawer for a fortune cookie. He read the fortune, frowned and threw it away. Who needs that: He who hesitates is lost, but it is better to be lost than dead. What kind of nonsense is that? He opened another ... and another and another, becoming increasingly anxious and annoyed. He had been bothered by the ambiguity of some of the previous fortunes, but now they were being downright negative. He reached for the last one and it too was the same. If he took the advice of the cookies he opened today he would go home and lock himself in a closet. Right now he wished he could do just that. He hated the idea of trying to close this deal feeling so nervous and negative. He frowned and looked at the pile of cookies and fortunes in his waste paper basket. What the hell was going on? Why was everything suddenly against him? Krist, he wished he could cancel the appointment! But if he did it would be all over. He would never get another chance. Not like this. He would not get the Corporate appointment. He had to see him today. But why was everything going wrong? He had lit his candles this morning. Why should this be happening to him? He looked through all his drawers for the third or fourth time hoping to find a stray fortune cookie, one that he had somehow overlooked, but to no avail. There just wasnt any left. He was completely out. And there was no way he could get anymore before going uptown. Unless he had an early lunch in the Chinese restaurant next door. He brightened, Yeah. Thats what I/ll do. Thats where it all started anyway. I/ll have a quick lunch and get uptown in plenty of time. He brushed the cookie crumbs from his suit and left his office.

Something told him that he was not being too wise having lunch here today, having had lunch in a Chinese restaurant yesterday, but he was forced to dismiss the thought. He would be careful. He wouldnt eat much. He wouldnt take a chance on being victimized by the Chinese restaurant syndrome. Not today, and a faint voice way in the back of his head said: Famous last words.

He ate the soup and a little of the chop suey and quickly grabbed the fortune cookie when the waiter brought it and crushed it and read the fortune, then stared at it: There are times when the wisest thing to do is nothing. He could not believe it. This was insane. He waved to the waiter and asked him if he could bring him another fortune cookie. He nodded and when he brought it Harry cracked it open and almost moaned aloud as he read the fortune. Another one. I must be dreaming. Somebody must be playing some sort of trick.

He called the waiter again and asked for a dozen fortune cookies. The waiter looked at him for many seconds, Harry said excitedly that he would pay for them, breaking into a forced smile and explaining that it was for a joke. Eventually the waiter shrugged and brought another dozen fortune cookies. Harry stared at them for a moment, the waiter glancing at him from time to time, talking to the other waiters, then shrugging and shaking his head. Harry took a deep breath and relaxed as best he could and got ready to open the first one, girding his loins as if he were about to dive off a hundred foot tower into a tank of water through flaming oil. He opened the first one, read it quickly, tossed it aside and went to the next, repeating the same routine, his knot of anxiety growing with each one, becoming more and more sick, until he had opened them all (all the waiters were watching by this time, scratching their heads) and he sat staring at the pile of broken cookies and crumpled fortunes. Harry was on the verge of tears. He could not believe this was happening to him. All the way to the very brink of something great and then the entire world suddenly turns on him. He hadnt done anything to anyone. He lit his candles every morning. Why should this happen to him? It wasn't fair. Goddam it, it wasnt fair! Im not going to put up with it! I/ll be damned if I will! NO!!!! He spoke the last word aloud as he brought his fist down, hard and loud on a pile of broken cookies, the plates and little bottles jumping and clanging, people suddenly silent, sitting still, forks suspended in air, looking first at each other, then turning around to find the source of the disturbance; the waiters too stopping in mid-motion, looking at Harry and blinking as Harry ground his hand into the cookies and shouted, Im not going to put up with it! Thats it! Harry continued to mutter to himself as he paid his bill, unaware that everyone was staring at him, commenting that he was as mad as a hatter.

Harry was full of energy when he entered Mr. Ralstons office. The first thing Mr. Ralston did was to inform Harry that he was very busy and did not have time for superfluities. That was just fine with Harry as he was well prepared and wanted to get on with it too. He presented all the figures quickly, giving Mr.

Ralston a copy of everything, noting the salient points, answering all questions easily and succinctly and when the meeting was concluded he left Mr. Ralstons office with the order.

When he got back Harry went directly to his office and plunked himself in his chair. By now his body was wet with perspiration and his insides were a turmoil of confusion and disbelief. He had the signed order right here but the fact seemed to be somewhere outside him. He knew it was real but it did not seem to have any pertinence to him, and the reality of the entire situation became increasingly vague the more he pondered it because he just could not believe it happened. How did it all come about? He could barely remember being in Mr. Ralstons office. He thought and thought and simply ended up increasing his confusion.

And what made it even more perplexing was the fact that he knew this would change his life. Every aspect of it. A house in Connecticut with trees and a garden. A summer place in Marthas Vineyard. Cars. A boat. Yeah . . . maybe a forty foot sloop and he would sail before the wind feeling the spray and breeze on his face . . .

But he would be functioning on the Corporate level now . . . .

The thought was frightening. How could he possibly function on that level? How could he possibly make a speech before the Board of Directors (the mere thought sent tremors through his mind and body) giving them progress reports . . . advising them of projected sales . . . O krist, thats right. I/d have to continue making deals like this. I/d have a position to maintain! How could I do it? This one was a fluke. Theres no way I can do this again . . . Jesus, the Board wouldnt be satisfied for long theyd want it done again and again and again . . .

O God, I cant do it. I could never take the pressure – he glanced at the pile of broken fortune cookies in his wastepaperbasket – I wouldnt know what to do. Being a salesman is one thing, but Corporate Staff . . . the responsibility . . .

and he/d be stuck with the house in Connecticut and the summer place in Marthas Vineyard and the boat and cars . . .   O God, no . . . no . . .

He felt icy cold and shivered as panic twisted itself through then around him, squeezing him tighter and tighter, making it almost impossible to breathe . . . He struggled to gulp air into his lungs, then leaned forward and rested his elbows on his desk and held his head, sinking deeper and deeper into his despair . . .

Then he noticed something in the newspaper on his desk At first it was a blur but something forced his attention to that area and he found he could not move his gaze away from it. He blinked his eyes until his vision cleared and he realized he was staring at the daily horoscope, his horoscope for today: Today is the day to assert yourself. Great opportunities are yours if you just take the bull by the horns. Dont take no for an answer. He read it over . . . then again . . . at first just the words got through, and then their meaning, his body becoming more and more erect as he read, his face relaxing into a smile . . .

then he slammed his hand down, hard, on the paper and jumped to his feet, Of course! Thats it! I knew it! I just knew it! I knew today was my day!!!! Thank God Im not superstitious or I might have let those damn cookies ruin my life. Now I know how to do it – tapping the paper – right there all the time. Haha, theres no way I can be stopped now! He snatched the signed contract from his desk and went to the Executive Wing to advise the President in person that he had wrapped up the deal. After all, he may just as well start getting used to his new neighborhood!!!!

A Penny for Your Thoughts

He didnt think of her breasts at first. He simply noticed how attractive she was. And too it was extremely unusual to see a young girl without makeup. She probably was no more than 18. He was waiting for the subway after work and she was standing among the crowd with a few friends. She wore a black coat and a black kerchief. Her skin appeared very white and her eyes were dark and sparkled. He kept glancing at her. He stood near them on the train and was surprised when they got off at his stop. He walked slowly and tried to listen to their conversation, but the only thing he heard distinctly was her name: Marie. A block from the station she said goodbye to her friends and turned along the avenue and he continued home.

The next morning he saw her on the station. He stood near her trying to determine the color of her eyes, but couldnt (at least not without being obvious) and was amazed again at her natural beauty, not glamorous, but quiet, exciting. They got off at DeKalb Avenue and he walked slowly up the stairs behind her and her girl-friends hoping he might see a bit more of her legs, but she held her coat tightly around her and with straining and falling behind as she climbed the stairs he was still only able to see her calves. They were very attractive though. Even with those flat slippertype shoes on. She turned at the exit and walked off in a different direction than the one he had to take, so he stood for a moment watching . . . then turned and went to his office.

He didnt see her that night on the platform. He looked around and had almost convinced himself that he should wait for another train, one that would be less crowded, but there was an area that was big enough for 3 or 4 people and the train remained there for a few seconds with the doors open and he felt guilty and conspicuous standing there when there was all that room and suppose someone he knew should ask him what he was waiting for or what if there should be some kind of a police investigation for some reason what could he say? And there are witnesses to prove there was room in the train – he stepped forward quickly just before the door closed.

After dinner he stretched out on the couch and tried to conjure up an image of Marie. All he could see was a vague outline, his wifes voice making it impossible to flesh out the image. He stopped trying and got up from the couch, went out to the kitchen and helped his wife with the dishes, his wife surprised, but saying nothing.

About 10 oclock he said he was going to bed as he was bushed from the extra work in the office and was relieved when his wife said, no, she wouldnt come to bed now, but would finish the ironing first. He lay in bed and thought of Marie. He thought of her dressed in a beautiful tight sheath with dark stockings, but the image continually blurred. He had never seen her with her overcoat off and without a kerchief around her head. Actually he didnt have the slightest idea of what her body looked like, only what he assumed from looking at her legs and face. She obviously wasnt fat, but he still didnt know *exactly* how she looked. How about her tits? She might be flatchested. . . . Cant really tell with that overcoat. NO NO! She must have a nice pair. Large and firm. Sure . . . She must . . .

He ate breakfast just a little faster the next morning wanting to be certain to get to the station in time to get the train she always took, but not too fast so his wife wouldnt ask questions. Marie was there on the platform and he got on the train with her and her friends and rode to work trying not to stare, but listening to her voice and watching from the side of his eye and hoping her coat would fall open when she reached up to adjust her kerchief, but it didnt. While still watching her coat and hoping, he looked at her face and noticed the small blemish on her right cheek, but it didnt bother him. It didnt affect her beauty. And anyway it was just a small spot. Probably temporary and nothing that would scar her skin. He did wish that she didnt go to work with her hair in curlers, though she does look much prettier than Alice with her hair set. Actually it was only the front she kept set. The back hung loose. It was long, wavy and very pretty. If she put something on it to make it blacker and shinier it would really be something, but it was very nice the way it was. Really nicer than Alices, but that was something else. He was just curious about this girl. She must be 10 years younger than him. It's just that shes unusually attractive. Good Lord, cant a guy look at a girl and find her attractive without something being made of it. Alice certainly wouldnt mind . . . It was their stop and they got off and he turned looking once more, then went to work.

When he mentioned the girl he saw on the platform to Alice he tried to do so with an *in passing* attitude, but he wanted to be certain he didnt overdo it. He was sure she didnt think twice about it as the conversation drifted to a natural tangent after he mentioned how attractive this girl was and it was a shame she didnt put her makeup on properly instead of smearing it all over. You know how these kids do it, and then they were talking about high school or something and he felt better, much better. Now when he thought about Marie he wouldnt feel guilty. And anyway, why should he?

He saw her every day, twice, for the next 4 days and he watched her the whole time from the moment he saw her on the platform until they parted at 3rd Avenue . . . still he didnt see them. And this was January. So long before spring and lighter coats that would be allowed to fall open and so much longer to summer when only dresses and blouses were worn– and he stared and stared . . . *Hello. I hope you dont think Im too forward, but Ive seen you every day for quite some time now and I am sure you have noticed that I have been staring at you. I suppose it is a little unusual to just speak to a girl on the subway like this, but it is just that you are so attractive* – a train came in and they got in and he tried to reach her, but couldnt get through the crowd or continue his imagined conversation; and then the train stopped and he got off and stayed a few feet behind and watched her and tried to go back to where they were on the platform and he was telling her how beautiful she is and she was about to smile (shyly perhaps) and tell him he was right, that she had noticed him looking at her and he would be able to understand (from her tone and attitude) that she was flattered – but he couldnt get back there and whenever he tried to isolate just them, alone, he suddenly tried to remember the color of Alices eyes. He tried pushing the thought from his mind, shoving it away with his hand, but there was felt no resistance and it just flowed around like an amoeba, an enormous amoeba; he tried gripping it; kicking it; dragging it; but the thought just floated and flowed. He even closed his eyes for a moment as he stood on a corner waiting for the light to change, but the thought wouldnt move so he stopped trying to keep it out of his mind and conjuring up his wifes eyes it slowly disappeared; then he tried to make his wifes eyes bigger and bigger so he could see what color they were, but he failed. It was impossible. But they must be blue. Shes so fair. They must be. They have to be. Blue Blue BLUE!!! Still he couldnt believe they were. But that doesnt mean anything. You know yourself how you forget things like that. But Maries eyes are brown. A deep dark brown. And they sparkle. Dont they? But thats different. How can you doubt I love Alice? I really know the color of her eyes. Its just trying to force it like this. Thats why I cant remember . . . .

Hello sweetheart. He bent and kissed Alices hair (of course theyre green. Its ridiculous. I knew) and asked her whats for supper.

⋍ He went to bed early again, giving some excuse about not feeling well, smoked a few cigarettes and thought of her. He wondered what would happen if he werent married, not that Im not happy after 4 years of marriage or anything, you know, but I just wonder. Academically so to speak. Id have a car of course – but I wouldnt be living here and would never have seen her anyway – have to start again. I live here – he put the cigarette out and rolled over on his side dismissing all the meaningless things that were ruining his thoughts. He was single and he had an apartment of his own near Fort Hamilton with a nice hi-fi, indirect lighting and even a small bar (Id have the money) and he knew her from work and they went out and stopped at his apartment for a nightcap – maybe they went to the Casino or some place on the Island – and he put on the radio and played soft music and when he gave her her drink he held her hand and kissed her and he slowly began to undress her and she was bashful and flushed slightly and he kissed her and reassured her and told her he loved her and she grabbed him and kissed him hard and he led her, gently, to the bedroom and they lay down and he felt her skirt under his fingertips and he played with her skirt for a few moments then the smoothness of her thigh and she turned, sighing, and the train came in and he held up his hand and pushed at it and tried to punch the hundreds of motormen, but it ran right through the room and through the bed and he held her and whispered, still trying to push the train, and all those damn people were walking by . . . O Goddam it! he slammed the door! slammed it again and again and again, running back to her and kissing her and slamming the door again, I love you, I LOVE YOU, frantically trying to unbutton her blouse and a large trailer truck went by and he struggled to get her blouse off and Alice asked him if he felt alright, Youre turning and tossing so much. Are you sure you feel alright honey? and he turned and mumbled something and lit another cigarette and she continued to talk as she undressed and he nodded and mumbled and smoked, hoping he hadnt blurted out something, and anyway its not like it was real and he didnt love Alice . . . o well . . . But its not really wrong. This is not at all like those guys who have girlfriends on the side. This is something different. Ive never been untrue to Alice. I even told Alice about her – goodnight sweetheart – Alice reached up and pulled the cord and the room was dark again and he put out his cigarette and tried to keep his mind blank, not wanting to fall asleep thinking about her and perhaps say something in his sleep . . . He couldnt get her out of his mind and kept waking with a start, listening for something and when he awoke about 3 or 4 he was so excited he tried waking Alice, but she didnt awaken when he touched her lightly so he stopped trying, afraid he might say something with his excitement and sleepiness, so he just lit another cigarette and thought about work or something . . . anything, until he felt calmer, then put out the cigarette and finally fell asleep.

He was exhausted in the morning and he told Alice to call the office and tell them he wouldnt be in, that he wasnt feeling well. He told her he might be getting the virus and thought it better to take it easy for a day or two than take a chance on getting sick. He stayed in bed all that day and the next, which was Friday, and just lolled around most of the weekend. On Monday he said he felt better and Alice suggested he wait an hour before going to work in order to avoid the rush hour, but he said that was ridiculous. Theres no need for any such thing. I can go at the regular time. Alice was stunned by his brisk manner and stared for a moment, then continued setting the table when he lowered his eyes.

He rushed to the station and didnt slow down until he saw Marie at the end of the platform. It seemed as if weeks had passed since he stood on the platform next to her and he was certain she had been aware of his long absence and probably wanted to talk to him. There certainly wouldnt be any harm in speaking to her – the train came in and it was unusually crowded and he pushed his way in and Marie and her girlfriends just did get in, the door hitting one girlfriend on the shoulder, and they screeched slightly at the difficulty and he smiled and almost spoke, but caught himself – yes, yes of course. Alices eyes are green and her hair is cut in a sortofa d.a. More people got on at the next stop and he was jabbed against her side and he thought it would be easy to simply let his arm rub against her breast or he could lower his hand and the next time there was a push his hand would rub against her ass and he looked and looked but he couldnt see. Incredible, but he still couldnt see. Still didnt know if she had a big pair or not. Not that that mattered either. Just a case of curiosity. No, no. Nothing like that. Dont be silly. I wouldnt really do it. Would be easy enough though. Especially in a crowd like this. It really would be an accident. But if I could just see how big they are. I mean . . . .

There seemed to be no way he could find out. Would he have

to wait until spring or even summer? It was ridiculous. Why in the name of Krist didnt she stop clutching her coat. It isnt that cold. She could let the goddam thing open in the subway. It was warm enough. If only it was a tight one, a fitted coat, then at least there would be an outline to see and allowing for the thickness of the coat you would have some idea of just how big her tits are. He didnt expect them to be gigantic (theres nothing wrong with Alices. Theyre not too small. Ive said that before. I dont really mind. That has nothing to do with it) just large and firm. She seemed to have nice wide hips. If she has a slim waist and a big pair ... all white and smooth and when she lays on her back theyd probably fall to the side slightly and her nipples will probably be rosy ... and the trains and people and trucks kept forcing him away from her and they parted at 3rd Avenue each night and he thought about it in bed, 4, 5 maybe more times he thought of waking Alice in the middle of the night, but he smoked, turned on his side and his thighs cramped and his stomach twinged ... and he kept looking and looking and they parted at the corner each morning after the light changed and she clutched that goddam coat and he looked and looked and he couldnt see and he didnt sleep and he was always keyedup and tensed and Alice knew it was the job and she didnt want to let him know she was upset worrying about him so she tried to ignore it and talked to him during mealtimes so he would relax enough to eat (he really wasnt eating much lately and lost weight) and she smiled and tried to be casual when asking him about work and his evasiveness confirmed her thoughts about the job fraying his nerves and still he looked and looked and Alice worried and he continued to lose weight and she thought of suggesting a visit to the doctor, but was still fearful of seeming alarmed and didnt want to upset him so after supper she suggested a movie. Its Friday and theres a good feature playing tonight. Its supposed to be very funny and you know how hard youve been working lately honey. Yeah, I guess I have, not knowing what she was talking about, but afraid to ask. It might relax you to sit in a movie. He nodded and they went to the movie and he sat watching and smoking and then he started chuckling, then laughing and he relaxed and stretched out his legs and Alice leaned against him and held his arm and glanced at him occasionally, and they laughed.

And then Marie was standing in the aisle, in front of him, looking up at the rear of the balcony and then seeing her friends she smiled and walked past him, up the aisle. At first he was a little surprised, but of course there was no reason why she shouldnt go to this movie. Then, of course, when she started to open her coat he tried to see her tits, but couldn't. All he could make out was that she was wearing a black sweater. And her hair wasnt straight and looked nice in the darkness of the movie. Then she was gone. Sitting somewhere behind him. He wondered if she noticed him. Dont imagine she saw the ring on Alices hand. Might be alright if she knew. Married men are more attractive to some women.

He concentrated on the movie, laughing and whispering to Alice and then Marie walked by with another girl. He really didnt notice until she had passed and was on her way down the stairs. He continued watching the movie but watched the staircase from the side of his eye. He felt his muscles tensing and made an effort to relax. He didnt want Alice to get any ideas. He fought his muscles. Watched the movie. The staircase. 15 maybe 20 minutes. He thought perhaps she had left. But of course that was silly. She just got here. And anyway, he did notice that she wasnt wearing her coat. He waited. And waited. Finally he heard their voices and they came to the top of the staircase, stood for a moment then walked past him and up the aisle. He looked, but the railing in front of him was on a level with her chest as she walked by and he was too amazed to try to look as they walked past him up the aisle. It was fantastic. Unbelievable. All he wanted to do was see how big her goddam tits were and this railings in the way. Howinthehell . . .

Maybe theyll come by again. If we were sitting back a row. How could I ask Alice to move. I insisted on sitting here to stretch out my legs. There might be something I could say. Better not. She might think it strange. Theyll come by again and when they go up the aisle I/ll be able to see. Maybe I should tell Alice thats the girl I told her about. She may have noticed me staring. No, I dont think so. A good kid that Alice. He looked at Alice and smiled and she smiled back and asked how he liked the show and he said good. Very good. Her smile broadened and she squeezed his arm and he waited for Marie to go by again trying to look behind him but they were all the way up and he couldnt see that far without turning completely around and looking deliberately and being obvious. He just sat, smoked, watched the movie and waited. He heard faint footsteps and voices and 3 girls passed and went down the stairs and Marie was one of them. He sat up higher in his seat and started turning his head slowly toward the aisle and adjusting his eyes, testing to see how large an area he could see without moving his head too far. He reached a point where he could see more than necessary while still, apparently, looking at the screen. He froze himself in the position and waited. His neck muscles started to stiffen and his eyes burned but he didnt move. He closed his eyes briefly then opened them and waited. When she came by he wouldnt have to move and he would see . . .

Then Alice tugged at his arm and pulled him toward her slightly. Would you go down and get me a pack of cigarettes honey. Im all out. He glared for a moment (after spending all that time getting ready and she might come at any minute) and almost yelled at her to get her own damn cigarettes. You should have made sure you had enough before we got here, but then he thought perhaps they arent in the Ladies Room and are downstairs at the candy counter. He mumbled a quick o.k. and dashed down the stairs to the candystand. They were standing around a soda machine talking. He bought the cigarettes then stood to one side and looked at them. She did have a nice pair. Not gigantic, just right. And her waist was beautifully slim and when she turned he could see that they were firm, really firm, and not just held up with a brassiere. Of course they might hang a little without a brassiere. Thats only natural. But they wouldnt sag. And her mouth was lovely. O, I bet she'd bite. Her thighs must be so smooth . . .

The girls dropped their cups in the bucket and started walking toward him. He turned and climbed the stairs two at a time and dropped back in his seat and handed the cigarettes to his wife, trying to breathe normally, and fixed his eyes on the proper spot. He sat and waited and when they climbed the stairs to their seats he watched them bounce – just slightly – and she passed so close he could smell the soap she had washed with and he could reach out and pat her ass. He stretched out and lit a cigarette and struggled with a conductor, a train and an usher that kept coming through the room but he kept closing doors and pulling down shades and she was naked on the bed and he kissed her and he turned in his seat and sat up and crossed his legs and was motionless and without thought for just a second then put his arm around Alice and rubbed his nose against her ear. She looked at him and smiled, kissed his cheek and snuggled closer to him and rubbed his arm, singing inside at seeing him relaxed and smiling and loving the way he caressed her cheek. She lifted his hand to her lips and kissed his fingertips. He put his arm around her, kissed her neck and said lets go home. But we havent seen the cartoons silly. I know hon, but lets go anyway. I want to talk to you. He caressed her neck with the tips of his fingers and looked into her eyes. Ah Harry, dont. Please dont. You know I cant do anything now.

He dropped his hands and stared at her for a moment then slammed back into his seat. O for Krist sake. Whats wrong Harry? Nothings wrong, goddam it. Nothing. Why don't you just leave me alone . . .

Liebesnacht

I dont want to talk about it anymore Harry.

What do you mean you dont want to talk about it anymore? Just like that the discussions over, wham, goodbye?

Her expression was stiff; her body as rigid as her attitude. She held the phone a few inches from her mouth and closed her eyes slightly and looked across the room at the wall and spoke very matter-of-factly. I see no reason to continue talking. You absolutely refuse to see my point of view and are unreasonably arbitrary about having your own way.

His eyes snapped open as wide as possible and he twisted and turned and paced back and forth as his arms flew in all directions forcing him to almost pursue the phone from time to time to be sure he could be heard. My way? Whatta you talking about? Ive taken you to see Star Wars twice already and now youre bugged because I dont want to see it again tonight. How in the hell does that make *me* arbitrary? Im willing to do anything you –

You see – her expression frozen in sternness – there you go again, trying to put the blame on me, trying to –

Blame, blame – he spun around and leaned so far back that he was looking at the ceiling over the mouthpiece of the phone – whats this blame? Im not looking for blame. Im just trying –

Youre just trying to make me feel like a fool for wanting to see the –

No no, I dont care how many times you see the goddam flick, I just want to take you –

You dont have to swear at me just to prove youre a man.

Prove Im a man? – shaking his head and rolling his eyes – all I wanted to do was take you to a party and you come on with this crazy bullshit about Star Wars and –

O now Im crazy. Thank you. Thanks a lot. Whats the matter, I attack your male ego?

I dont believe this – slapping his head – I dont believe it. Having the rag on is one thing but this is ridic–

Thats right, lets hide behind that and try and make me feel guilty or ridiculous or –

Holy Krist, every time I talk to you lately its the same thing, the same nonsense.

O now its nonsense if I dont want to constantly give in to you and your whims –

Whims? What kind of whims? I just want to take you to a party and you –

Harry, I dont want to talk about it further. You absolutely refuse to see my point of view.

Refuse to – CLICK – What? What? – staring at the phone, holding it at arms length – whatta ya doin? Youre out ya head you crazy bitch, you . . . you . . . ah, who needsya. He slammed the receiver on the cradle and then slammed the phone on the table and left the house.

He stomped his way up the street trying to pound his anger into the pavement, clenching and unclenching his jaw and fists, shaking his head and almost yelling out loud as his head continued the battle, trying to force a semblance of sense into Marys head with the sheer energy of his anger because it didnt make any sense. No matter how you slice it it just doesnt make any sense. She must have some kindda bug up her ass. I call and ask her if she wants to go out to dinner before the party and she suddenly says she doesnt want to go – his mind assumed a falsetto voice – I want to see Star Wars. I mean whats with this Star Wars? and whats with all this contrary shit lately? starting arguments over nothing. Make a date and then cancelling at the last minute or complaining about where we go and what we do after I ask what do you want to do???? If you dont like this and you dont like that then what in the hell do you wanna do? – the falsetto again – O you decide Harry. I cant make up my mind. Yeah, an everything I decide is no good. We go to a restaurant and all of a sudden the lighting is no good. The lighting, right? Who cares about the food? all of a sudden its the lights that are important. You hungry go to Nathans, they got nice lights. We go to Fire Island for a weekend and its too far to the beach. Can you believe it? Too far to the beach!!!! The whole fucking island is only 3 feet wide and its nothing but beach. Its crazy, crazy. I dont get it. All she wants to do is break my balls – falsetto squeaks in – If I break them its because you put them on the chopping block for me. Harry started waving his hand then selfconsciously stopped and jammed it in his pocket. Eh, who needs it. I need this like I need a hole in the head. I must be crazy to bug myself over that broad. How did I ever get hooked into her anyway???? Forget it. Who needs it. Almost a year. One broad. I must be nuts. Harry quickened his pace even more to outdistance any reply his mind might make, falsetto or otherwise, and continued to try to outdistance his head as he automatically eased his way between the traffic as he crossed the avenue, then started to slow his pace as he neared STEVES, a neighborhood bar where his friends hung out.

It wasnt until he stopped, just inside the door, and felt the wave of cool air that he realized he was hot and flushed. He suddenly became aware of the sweat rolling down his sides and back and burning his eyes. He wiped his face quickly with his handkerchief as he looked around for a second, then walked toward his friends.

Hey Harry, whatta you doin here?

Whatta ya say Ron – he looked at Larry and Kelly – whats happening? Larry shrugged, Wanna beer? Sure, why not. Larry leaned over the bar, Hey Bob, give lover boy a beer. They all chuckled.

Kelly drained his glass and put it on the bar, May just as well put a head on this. He turned to Harry, How come youre here? Its – squinting at the clock on the wall – about 8:03 and its Saturday night.

Yeah, wheres Mary?

Harry tossed his head back, Eh, forget it.

What happened man, she split?

Dont ask. You wouldnt believe it – Harry grabbed his glass and gulped half of it and sighed as he put it down. – Krist thats good. I didnt realize how thirsty I was. He finished his beer and put some money on the bar, Hey Bob, giveus another round.

The door opened and Wally, Artie and Matt came in and stopped halfway down the bar. Harry barely noticed them out of the corner of his eye, and then Wally put his hands on the bar and Harry frowned and turned his head and looked at the cast on Wallys thumb and around his wrist and the wire going across the tips of his fingers. What happened to Wally?

O man, it was somethin else.

His brother.

Mikey no legs?

Yeah. Drunk outta his mind. You know how he gets.

Yeah – nodding his head.

It happened just a coupla hours ago. No legs comes in an hes bouncin off the walls and knockin people all over and Wally tries to takeim outside and Mike is blitherin about the Nuns and arithmetic – they all start chuckling and nodding their heads – You know, when he goes off he goes off. He dont know nobody.

Yeah you aint kiddin. Hes really fuckin crazy when hes bombed.

So he suddenly grabs Wallys thumb and just bends it back, real quick, and you could hear it snap a block away.

It was really weird because he looked like he was pushin down on a lever or somethin. I mean you could see that he didnt know what he was doin.

Or who Wally was. Just a quick snap. And he just walks out and Wally and Matt and Artie are staring at Wallys thumb, an then everybody in the joint is staring at it until Bob pours him a good stiff shot and after he drinks it Wally almost falls on his ass. He grabs his wrist and starts rockin back and forth and Matty runs out and grabs a cab and they went down to the emergency.

I guess it wasnt too crowded, they got back pretty fast. At least for that joint.

Yeah, well its early yet. The night is young.

And youre so beautiful. Kelly pinched Larrys cheek and they all chuckled and reached for their beers.

Mikey no legs was in the cellar of his apartment building. His parents had lived there for 10 years before he was born, and for 5 years before Wally was born. And they lived there still. The four of them. And they were still the supers, a job that was much easier since the furnace was converted to oil quite a few years ago: no coal to shovel, no ashes to carry out, no fire to shake and bank and worry about. But there was still the garbage cans to put out, a job Mike had been doing for almost 20 of the 28 years of his life.

Mike started by helping Wally with the cans, always wanting to follow his big brother. He idolized Wally and begged him to let him help with the cans, and he did. At first Wally took most of the weight, patting his brother on the back and telling him he was a real good helper. Then Mike was taking one up all by himself, tugging on the handle as the can banged against the stone steps. Eventually he was able to pick up the can and carry it up the steps, and then with the passing of a few more years, he simply picked up one in each hand and almost ran them up the stairs.

The same occurred with the much heavier cans of ashes, Mike developing incredible strength.

Now there were no ashes. But they were still the supers and Mike carried the garbage cans up the same immortal steps only slightly worn by cans and shoes.

Although he was called no legs, it was not an accurate description. It was simply that he had a large barrel chest that carrying the cans had made even larger, and his legs appeared too short for his body.

He wasnt exceptionally violent or quiet, just sort of unobtrusively there, except when he got crazy drunk. Fortunately he only got drunk periodically, and then it was only occasionally that he got violent, when some twisted message tripped through his drunken body to his brain and voices burned his head and he couldnt scream them quiet, and, from time to time, things would appear either without or within his head that he had to defend himself against.

Mike sat on the floor leaning against the wooden wall of a storage room, a bottle of wine on the floor beside him and a small transistor radio. From time to time he would take a drink, then turn the dial from one end of the band to the other trying to find the ballgame. He knew there was one somewhere, but where???? He looked at the radio, his head swaying back and forth, eyes half closed, barely able to see the radio in the dimness of the cellar, Where are ya ya son of a bitch? Eh? Wheres those fuckin Mets? He continued spinning the dial eliding from one station to another, one song to another, one announcer to another, the rock rolling into the pop as his finger continued pushing the small wheel and suddenly a soprano screeched and he twisted the radio, Shut up bitch. He squeezed the radio and pulled his hand back, but then lowered it slowly and put the radio back on the ground. Fuck it. Who needs this shit. He took another drink of wine then slowly curled onto the floor, pillowing his head on an arm, and slept.

The game was on in STEVES and the guys at the bar looked at it from time to time. Harry and his friends decided they would chugalug a beer every time there was a double play or a home run. After two innings of neither one they extended it to include strike outs, stolen bases, runners caught trying to steal, bases on balls, scoreless half innings, and every third out. After six innings they also included the seventh inning stretch. Half an hour after the game ended, they had forgotten the score and werent too certain who won or who had played.

To Harry it seemed like the best game he had ever seen. He couldnt remember when he had laughed so much or so hard. The Mets were always good for a laugh, but tonight was something special. He felt loose, relaxed. He hadnt realized it until now, but this was exactly what he needed, a night out with the boys ... drinking beer, watching a ball game, swapping stories and having some good laughs. He was feeling good ... great. He staggered slightly, but only for a second, when he pushed himself away from the bar and started toward the mens room . . . again. One thing about that fuckin beer, it sure goes through you. He slowly worked his way to the mens room and leaned against the wall and looked down at the cake of ice in the urinal. The flushometer never worked and so everyone in STEVES indulged in the art of ice writing. He had started to carve his initials on his previous trips but his efforts had been obliterated by others who had no respect for his artistic endeavors and were happy to just piss indiscriminately on the ice while sighing, Ahhh, this is the pause that refreshes; or just trying to cut the piece in half (half a piece is better than none, hahaha) or just chip away at an edge. No class. No fucking class. Harry was determined that he would carve at least one clear, clean, recognizable H in the ice before the night was over and so, although there was a pressured urgency to his need to urinate, he squeezed his joint so just a thin stream of urine came out and carefully carved an almost near perfect (to him) H in the ice, still leaning against the wall with one hand and ignoring the splashing and splattering. When he finished he leaned back and looked with satisfaction at his initial and started to shake the final drops but stopped and moved so they would not fall on the results of his work and directed them to the corner of the urinal, a series of elipses going directly down the drain, not passing Go, not collecting two hundred dollars. He zipped his fly and stood swaying slightly in front of the urinal, smiling and nodding to the compliments he was hearing in his head. He wished he had a Polaroid camera so he could take a picture of it. Never see it again. Nobody/d believe it. Between the heat and all those assholes pissin all over it it wont be here long. Maybe he should just stay here and watch it slowly melt and stand in front of the urinal so nobody else could fuck it up. Naaa . . . shit, that aint no good. Anyway, Im fuckin thirsty an—

Ya finished?

Yeah. Harry took another few steps back.

Thank Krist. I gotta piss like a bandit. He sighed as there was a sudden flood of urine on the rocks, Ahhhhh, the pause that refreshes.

Harry stood for a moment, then blinked and shrugged and left, Dont get ya feet wet.

Yeah, hahahaha.

A fresh beer was waiting for Harry when he rejoined his friends. Comeon Harry, chugalug.

What for this time?

Who the fuck knows.

They chuckled and laughed, then controlled it just enough to drain their glasses, Harry having visions of a beautiful gothic H engraved in the ice.

Mike stirred, twisted his body, his head, then slowly sat up and looked around the darkened cellar, unable to see more than a foot or two away. He carefully moved his hand along the floor until he found his bottle, then picked it up. He tried to look at it but could see nothing of the contents so he shook it slightly and was relieved and happy to hear something splashing around inside. He took a long drink and closed his eyes and concentrated on the warm glow spreading within him, and smiled because he knew there was at least one good drink in the bottle, maybe more. He licked his lips and took another drink and when that had settled in he finished off the few remaining drops. He leaned against the wall as the wine continued on its journey and slowly a few things clicked into place. He knew where he was. He didnt have to be able to see to know he was in the cellar. He sat quietly for a few minutes listening to the sounds of the street, the sounds telling him that it wasnt too late, there were still people walking and talking so the bars must still be open. He jammed his hand in his pocket and felt some money. Thank Krist. He rubbed his head and his face. Must still be Saturday. Probably Saturday night. Yeah. Must be. Hope the fuck the bars are still open. He slowly stood up, leaning against the wooden wall, tested his legs, then paced himself to the stairs, feeling his way through the dark, able to walk just as freely and rapidly in the dark as in daylight, having spent so many hours, and having made so many trips, from where he was to the stairs that led to the street. Faint light from the street lamp near the top of the stairs cast a slanted shadow across the sidewalk and he stood at the top of the stairs for a moment, blinking, looking around, seeing lights on in most of the houses and feeling secure that there was still time to have fun.

He rotated his shoulders a few times as if loosening them up from heavy work, or getting ready for it, then started walking down the street, his pace quickening as he felt steadier on his feet.

Kelly was squinting slightly as he spoke to Harry, One thing you cant do is let a broad break ya balls – everyone was nodding – Thats right man. Ya gotta keepem in their place or they/ll shove it in and break it off.

Yeah, yeah, I know man – they were all unsteady on their feet and leaned heavily against the bar for support while trying to look nonchalant – gettin laid aint worth all that bullshit.

Ya goddamn right. Ya gotta letem know whos the fuckin boss – they were nodding wisely – hey, I aint bullshittin man – I know man. Im right withya Larry – they start comin on with that, do it my way or else, bullshit an ya gotta givem their walkin papers.

Hey, right on man. Take it from me, ya either slapem down or cutem loose.

Harry straightened as much as possible while still supporting himself on the bar and looking cool, Hey, I tolder where to shove her bullshit – shaking his head – I dont understand why shes runnin these fuckin games down all of a sudden.

O man, you know how these fuckin broads are, shes probably ballin some other cat but wants to keep you around in case it dont work out – they all nodded very wisely.

Yeah, thats their schtick man.

Well, I/ll tellya one thing – grabbing his crotch – this is one pair a balls she aint gonna put no strings around, or any other broad!

Hey!

Right on!

They all laughed and poked each other on the shoulder and

finished their beers and banged their glasses on the bar for Bob. Their laughter quickly dropped to faint chuckling as Mikey no legs came into the bar, stopped just inside the door and looked around.

Mike was feeling pretty good by the time he pushed the door open. The rest had refreshed him and the wine he drank before leaving his cellar had revitalized him. He was in the mood for fun, and did not notice that there was a sudden and prolonged decrease in laughter and conversation immediately he entered, the juke box suddenly seeming very loud. He smiled and walked to the bar and waved at Bob who started gingerly toward him, watching Mikes eyes for any hint of trouble. Whatta ya say Bob, giveus a beer, eh? Bob smiled and relaxed when he realized Mike knew who he was and seemed to be alright. He put the beer in front of Mike, smiling, picking up the proper change. Wally been in tonight?

Bob looked at him for a moment, having been behind the bar when Mike had been in earlier in the evening and broke Wallys thumb. He had seen Mike crazy drunk many times and knew he never remembered what happened so he just shrugged, He was in earlier but left.

Yeah? Who was he with?

I dont know – shrugging – maybe Matt and Artie.

Mike nodded and Bob went to the other end of the bar and the men resumed their previous conversations, the laughter growing in volume and the juke box receding to its proper place. The tension continued to decrease, rapidly, as Mike drank his beer He looked around and noticed Harry and the others and smiled at them and picked up his glass and walked toward them.

They were leery of drinking with Mike after what had happened earlier that evening. O shit, no legs is coming over.

Thats okay Ron, just cool it.

He looks pretty straight, maybe he slept it off.

I fuckin well hope so, I dont need anymore shit tonight.

Whatta ya say guys, whats goin on?

Eh – shrugging – you know Mike.

Same ol thing. The Mets lost again.

No shit? Krist, whats with those guys? I missed the game tanight – shrugs – big deal, eh? He chuckled and the others smiled cautiously. Mike finished his beer and put the empty glass on the bar, Comeon, drink up. I/d rather buy one than be one, eh? Mike laughed and the others relaxed and finished their beers.

They continued drinking and laughing, getting a little drunker with each round, everything that had happened earlier in the evening dissolved by the alcohol and unable to dim the increasing joy that each drink brought.

Then Wally came in. Larry nudged Ron and nodded toward the door as Wally stopped and looked at Mike who had just finished a beer and was wiping his mouth with the back of his hand. He saw Wally and his face opened in a quick, wide smile and he waved at him, Hey Wally, comere, Youre just in time for Harry to buy a drink. Mike laughed and walked to meet his brother and put an arm around his shoulder, Where ya been? ya missing all the fun. Bob was in the process of bringing beers for everyone and they all quieted and waited to see what would happen. Mike was happy and chuckling and pushed the beers along the bar to everyone, then picked up his and looked at his brother, Drink up, the brewery needs the barrels. Mike laughed, then took a drink and when he put his glass back on the bar he looked down and noticed his brothers hand. His face fell into a look of bewilderment and he stared at the cast and wire, What happened Wal? What the fuck happened? He finally looked up into Wallys face, his concern bringing tears to his eyes.

Wally knew that he would be seeing his brother sooner or later and had been trying to prepare himself for the confrontation, but even now did not know what he was going to say. Mike always looked to him for answers, for help, and Mike loved him. Mike had never hurt Wally before, but he had gotten into fights when he was crazy drunk, and never remembered them, and when he came to Wally was always there to help Mike through the remorse and guilt when he found out what he had done, or to protect him from the truth. But now Wally didnt know what to do. If he told him somebody did it to him he would want to know who, and if Wally didnt give him a name sooner or later Mike would decide that somebody walking the street did it and might try and kill them. Sooner or later Mike was bound to get crazy drunk again. And he sure as Krist couldnt tell him he just fell, even Mike wouldnt buy that. Wally didnt know what in hell to do. What would happen if he told Mike the truth? Shit! Wally loved his kid brother. He had told him a thousand fuckin times not to drink and Mike always swore he never would again, but eventually Mike had a beer with the guys, and sooner or later that led to another crazy drunk and trouble, and Wally felt that this would lead to the kind of trouble no one could get Mike out of, that some day he would kill somebody and wouldnt even know he did it. Wally looked into his brothers eyes and saw tears behind the sadness in them and felt Mikes pain, a pain so much more terrible than the pain Wally had felt in his thumb, and that would grow each time he looked at Wallys hand.

Mike lowered his gaze and once again stared at the cast and the tip of the thumb sticking in the air, the wire going from the tip of one finger to the other. It not only pained him to look at it, but it confused him too. The only thing Mike could see or think about was his brothers hand. He slowly reached down and touched the cast with the tip of his finger, gently, tentatively, as if it were alive and had feelings, like a child touching a turtle for the first time not knowing if he might kill it by pushing too hard on the shell. He stroked and patted it then held it gently in both hands and lifted it – the juke box suddenly went silent and those who knew Mike and Wally watched them until the music once more blared from the multicolored machine – and held it as if he were holding a baby for the first time, Who did it Wally? Who did it? Its nothing Mike. Forget it. Wally took his hand out of Mikes and smiled at him reassuringly. Who did it Wally – his voice louder and more anxious – I/ll killim. Take it easy Mike for Krists sake – Wallys anxiety mounting – its nothin ta get fucked up about. Mike put his arm around Wallys neck, I swear ta God Wally – his voice full of tears – Aint nobody gonna fuck with ya. Aint nobody gonna hurt ya. Wally put his hands on Mikes shoulders, then quickly yanked his injured one down. Im tellin ya Mike ta drop it. Just drop it, okay? Mike was crying and almost hanging on Wallys neck, I cant. I cant let somebody hurtya like that an get away with it. I dont give a shit how fuckin big he is or how fuckin many, I/ll getem. I swear on our Mothers head Wally I/ll – Wally shook his head and finally looked Mike in the eye and spoke as gently as he could through his confusion and fear, You did it Mike. Mike just stared, mouth hanging open, head shaking no. Yeah Mike. Earlier. Right here. Mikes mouth was still hanging open and his head shaking, I couldnt Wally, I couldnt – he looked at Wallys hand and more tears rolled down his cheeks. The tension and apprehension of the evening and the years, the worry and concern for his kid brother knocked down all the walls Wally had built and he almost cried as he shook Mike with his good hand, Jesus Krist Mike, I keep tellinya not to drink like that but you wont fuckin listen to me, I keep tellin ya every fuckin time – Mike was still shaking his head and crying, Wallys voice cracking with an occasional sob – to just take a couple a drinks an cool it but you gotta get stoned an go fuckin crazy and worry the shit outta me until I dont know whats comin down sometimes – Wally shook Mike again as he sobbed – I dont wanna see ya fucked up like this, Mike, Jesus Krist, I dont know what the fuck ta do for ya – Mike was once again staring at Wallys hand, his tears falling from his cheeks onto the cast – listen to me for Krists sake Mike, eh? ya listen to me this time???? Mike slowly raised his head and blinked his eyes, his expression so sorrowful Wally wanted to cry and just hug his brother – Does it hurt Wally, I mean did it, – Mike shrugged – hurt . . . real bad? Wally was smiling and shaking his head, Naw, naw, I dont feel nothin Mike. They fixed it up one, two, three and – Im sorry Wally, Jesus Krist Im sorry – agony ringing in his voice –I/ll break my own – grabbing his thumb – if thatll help, I – Wally grabbed his hand, No Mike, for Krists sake comeon, eh? Wally smiled and tried to look reassuringly at his brother who stared soulfully at him, I really did it Wally? Wally nodded, Yeah Mike. But its alright. I – I honest ta God did it? Wally nodded his head and gently touched his brother on the shoulder. Mike looked at

Wallys hand, head shaking, then put his arms around Wally and hugged him and cried into his shoulder, the others shuffling awkwardly, some averting their eyes trying to ignore the scene, those who didnt know them assuming they were just a couple of maudlin drunks. Mike suddenly turned from his brother and started pounding the bar with his hand, I cant believe it, I cant fuckin believe it – the others stiffened until Mike stopped and just leaned over the bar, head hanging. Wally put an arm around his kid brothers shoulder, Why dont we go out an get some air? After a few seconds Mike raised his head, nodded, and continued to look at the floor as they left the bar, their friends automatically following.

Mike sat on a car fender, Wally standing next to him. The others stretched. I forget what fresh airs like after a few hours in that joint.

Yeah. Its the fuckin air conditioner.

Yeah, it smokes too much. They all chuckled.

Man, its some night, eh?

Yeah, its really nice out.

Why dont ya leave it out?

Because I dont want anybody steppin on it – they started horsing around and Wally suggested they walk and put his hand on his brothers shoulder, Mike still looking at the ground, shaking his shoulders occasionally in response to the voices that were constantly dinning in his head. From time to time he would look at Wally and tell him he was sorry and Wally would tap him on the shoulder and tell him to forget it, its alright. No more Wally. I swear. No more. And they continued walking, leaving the avenue and walking along the path in the park area bordering the parkway, Harry, Ron, Kelly and Larry, once more feeling the effects of the nights drinking, joking and kidding around as they walked, Mike hearing their laughter and resenting it, not because he didnt want them to be happy, but because he wanted their laughter to somehow ease his pain, the pain that grew in gnawing knots within him, twisting his body and mind with tension, pain that was magnified by his guilt and overwhelming remorse, a pain that increased as he fought accepting the truth that he had broken his brothers hand, yet deep within him he knew he had. The truth continued to settle in and grow and be accepted and as it did Mikes agony increased because he didnt want it to be true. He didnt want to have done that to his brother. He had gotten into fights and didnt remember them, but he didnt give a shit about that. What the fuck did he care about those hardons? But how could he have done that to Wally? How? – hitting his head with his hands – How? How???? How could it happen? He didnt want to hurt his brother and the more he tried to figure what happened the more intense the pain and confusion became, and the more the pain grew the more he tried to figure out what happened and he kept getting deeper and deeper into a black nausea that twisted itself from his gut up to his throat threatening to make him puke, and up to the top of his head until it felt like it was about to be fuckin ripped open, and he was powerless to do anything about the pain or the cause of the pain, all he could do was be victimized by it and be a part of the process without having any control, flailing impotently at the process and pain and trying to wish it all away: everything that had happened, the entire evening, and he kept telling himself that if he could only remember what had happened he could somehow change it, make believe it never happened, but then he would look at Wallys hand and the truth would descend on him like a dull and rusty guillotine and all he could feel was the crushing pain of dying without the release of death, and so he continued walking along the path, watching his feet and the shadow of Wallys hand, hearing painfully the laughter of the others

and then he became vaguely aware of another sound that worked its way through their laughter and the sounds of their walking, the sound of cars passing along the parkway, and the screeching in his head; it was the sound of chuckling and giggling and words that were barely audible but the sound was undeniably happy . . . yeah, thats what the voices said, they said they were happy. He couldnt figure the words out for shit but the voices said they were happy. He raised his head and noticed a young couple in the distance walking in their direction across the grass that sloped to the parkway. They passed through the cone of light from a streetlamp and he could see a guy and a girl, his arm around her waist, slowly walking, their voices happy, happy, and when they passed from the relative brightness near the lamp to the misty aura of the light they stopped and kissed and were quiet for a few moments ... and then their happy voices started up again and saying Krist knows what to each other. Mike watched them from the corner of his eye for a few minutes, then raised his head slightly, not wanting anyone to see what he was doing, and kept his eyes trained on them as they approached, ten feet or so off the path, and as he watched, seeing them more and more distinctly as they got nearer, his head got quieter and the grinding pain started to subside and a new excitement wormed its way through his tensed body, and as they drew abreast of them he stopped and watched them, Wally and the others stopping and looking at Mike.

Mike continued watching them then suddenly turned and looked around and ran to the fence and found an old, splintered piece of 2 x 4, and holding it like a club he walked toward the young couple and as he passed the guys he told Wally, Comeon, youre gonna get laid – and continued down the slope toward the couple. Wally and the others stood still for a moment, Mikes words not registering until they heard him yell at them – COMEON, IM GONNA GETYA LAID WALLY – the couple stopping and turning and looking at Mike as he descended on them waving the 2 x 4 – Ya betta get outta here asshole unless ya wanna get ya head bashed in. Were gonna fuck the ass off that cunt – and Mike laughed a sick laugh and the guy stepped forward in front of the girl and started looking around for a way to run when he noticed the other guys running toward them, screaming, MIKE! MIKE! ITS WALLY! Comeon Wally, Im gonna get ya fucked – and the girl started screaming and her boyfriend pushed her and told her to run but she could only hold on to him and scream as Mike stood in front of him waving the 2 x 4 and a couple of guys came up behind him and grabbed the club and a guy with a cast on his hand stood in front of the guy with the club saying something and someone else came over and told him to take his girl and beat it, and the guy put his arms around the trembling girl and they trotted then ran up the slope to the path and to the street and Wally continued to try to reason with Mike who seriously wanted to get a piece of ass for his brother, I mean, what the fuck Wally, it/ll take your mind off ya hand, right? and Wally nodded and did his best to smile as the others stood nervously around wondering if the cops would be there soon and if they would all suddenly end up in the fuckin slammer and wanting very much to get the fuckin hell outta there but didnt want to leave their friends so they stayed and Wally told Mike that he was tired, Its late Mike. I dont feel like gettin laid, okay? But she was a real doll Wally. She probably give ya a good blow job. Yeah, yeah, Mike, but not now, okay? Im fuckin beat Mike an Im tired of all this fuckin shit, ya hear me – his voice getting louder and angrier – I just want to go fuckin home and sleep and forget about this whole fuckin night – Mike nodding his head, Okay, okay, Wally, I didnt mean nothin – Good because Im goin home and I dont give a shit what you do – Wally turned and started walking rapidly – Ive had it with your bullshit. Okay Wally, no offense. Mike quickly caught up with Wally, the others following a few feet behind, hoping to Krist they could get rid of Mike and go back to STEVES and pick up where they left off before Mike fucked up the night. Mike had to almost run to keep up with Wally who refused to look at him or talk to him, and once again the pain and the voices started twisting him, creating a pressure inside that threatened to blow the top off his skull and he tried to vent it by pounding his feet on the pavement but it not only did not relieve the pressure, it seemed to increase it, and soon Mike was having trouble seeing properly as the anxiety caused his head to shake and his vision to blur and he kept telling his brother he was sorry and Wally kept walking rapidly and when they turned a corner they passed a newsstand and Mike suddenly screamed and yanked and tugged the hundreds of pounds of newsstand and eventually wrestled it off the ground and heaved it through the plate glass window of the store, still screaming, his screams piercing through the sound of the broken glass that thundered to the street in the late night stillness, and when the glass had stopped falling Mike still screamed and when he ran out of breath he inhaled and screamed again and the guys stopped and stared, wanting to run like hell but afraid to leave Wally alone with Mike and finally Mike stopped screaming as a head occurred in the window above the store and Wally grabbed Mike and they quickly disappeared around the corner as a voice from the window wanted to know what the hell was going on and the others went around the corner and ran along the avenue as Mike quietly followed Wally home.

Harry and his friends continued walking rapidly, toward STEVES, but just before they got there Harry said he didnt feel like drinking anymore and left them, wanting to be alone.

Harry walked down the street not certain where he was going or what he was going to do. He didnt feel like going home so he thought he would just walk around and maybe get his head cleared a bit. He had gone through so many emotions in the last few hours that he wasnt sure how he felt about anything. He wasnt even sure he knew what had happened. He walked along the quiet, tree-shadowed street and suddenly became aware of an urgent need to pee. He stood in the shadows of a tree between two cars and sighed with relief, then chuckled as he remembered the Gothic H he was going to carve in the ice. Shit, it was good to feel his face smile. That crazy Mikey no legs got him so fucked up it seemed like years since he laughed even though he knew it was just a short time ago they were laughing and having a ball . . . Yeah, I dont need her to have a good time. I had more laughs tonight then Ive had in a long time. He continued walking down the breezeless street, wiping his forehead with the back of his hand, suddenly aware of the humid heat. He took a deep breath, Yeah, a lot of laughs . . .

No breeze.
Not even a hint of one. His place would be like an oven. Even with the fan. Maybe I shouldve gone back to STEVES with the guys. A lot cooler. Couldve had a few more laughs. O well . . . shit . . . . He heard the sound of a tugboats horn and then another vessel answering and thought of the pier. Yeah. It/d be cooler there, a hell of a lot cooler. And quiet. Probably deserted this

time a night. Yeah, good idea. There was a slight spring to his step now, now that he knew where he was going, a destination clearly in mind, a purpose to his walking.

He walked to the end of the pier and sat down. He was heated from the walk, but there was a breeze, faint but refreshing on his face and arms. He sat quietly and allowed his body to cool down, enjoying the breeze and looking across the bay at the splotches of light on the shore lines, and the little dots of lights of the small harbor craft. He could only make out two ships anchored. Only two. And not much happening on the piers. Not like it used to be. He could remember when the harbor was always active and full of all kinds of ships but now there aint much goin on. Even the 69th Street ferry is gone. Even the old slips are gone. He looked down the pier where the ferry slips used to be, then at the Veranzanno Bridge that made the ferry a memory. Krist, what a gasser that was. Especially on a night like this. Ride to Staten Island, then over to the Battery and back all the way around again and just lean on the rail and feel the breeze and watch the water roll away from the sides of the ferry ... Jesus that was great. Natures air conditioning. And they had the guy playing the accordion and singing songs and that bootblack. Jesus, he mustta been there for ever. Wonder what that son of a bitch is doin now. Shit. Aint the same anymore. All changed. Ah, what the hell. She wants to play it that way what do I care. She has a bug upper ass that one, a bug upper ass. She/ll get over it. Probably ... How can you be so goofy for a movie??? Yeah, I guess ya cant. Must be something. He shrugged and looked again at the shorelines of Manhattan, Jersey, and Staten Island, watching a ferry going to the Battery. They should bring back the ferry for the summer. Everybody and his brother would want to ride it on a night like this. Just for July and August. Ah well, at least the piers still here. For now. Good ol 69th Street pier. Wonder how old the son of a bitch is? Had a lot of fun here. Right around this spot too. Learned to fish here. Tommy cods, eels, some crabbin. Had a lot a fun here when we were kids. Yeah, some good times ... Yeah, good times.

O, what the fuck – his stomach suddenly

felt hollow and sick – Rons right, shes ballin some other guy . . .
So its over, whats the big deal? She aint the first . . . or the last.
Got myself in a little too deep. Big deal. Fuck it. He looked down
at the dark water and the bits of debris floating out on the ebbing
tide, the undertow creating sudden and ephemeral whirlpools
around the end of the pier. He looked out a few yards from the
corner of the pier. Used to be a mud hole out there. Get your line
in there an you always got a bite. Pop used to be able to cast right
there and always got a good sized eel. Probably still a good spot
. . . Maybe. Might even be the same water . . . goes out and comes
in, out and in . . . back and forth . . . Ah screw it. In a month I
wont even remember her name . . . Probably.

He stared at the
water and the currents eddying around the pilings. Probably the
same

water

probably

The Sound

His eyes opened and he stared at the wall. The nightlight flickered and shadows jumped eerily around the 9 x 6 room. He lay still and listened. What woke him? He listened for a sound . . . Nothing. He looked up at the window. Darkness. There was no hint of dawn. Moving only his eyes, he looked up at the ceiling light. Only the flickering nightlight burned. What time was it? Had he slept one hour? Five hours? No way to tell. He lay on his side and slowly, unconsciously, pulled his legs up to a foetal position as he desperately clutched his pillow. His eyes started to tear as he continued staring at the flickering light, feeling the shadows float through the room. He blinked. His eyes filled with water and when he opened them the light shimmered and the room rolled slowly like a small boat on deep swells. The walls pulsated and undulated, threatening to close in on him. He shivered and blinked rapidly until his eyes dried. The room stilled. Still he heard nothing . . . the silence hostile.

Something awakened him, but what? A dream? He tried remembering . . . Nothing. It couldn't have been a dream . . .

He stared at the wall and the leaping shadows, straining to hear something . . . anything. There was only silence, heavy, ominous. Suddenly he became aware of painful cramps in his hands. He forced his hands open. At first they resisted and continued clutching his pillow. But slowly, painfully, his fingers straightened as he concentrated on the effort. He looked at his hands as the pain slowly subsided. Suddenly he jerked his head up, his vision blurring, wondering why he had bolted up. His body tensed even more as he listened intently . . .

Then he heard it. Or did he? It was so faint he couldn't be certain. Was this a dream? Was he still sleeping???? No. He must be awake. The pain in his hands; the flickering light and eerie shadows were real. They *had* to be real! He *had* heard that sound. He was sure of that. Wasn't he? It must have been real . . . He straightened his legs slowly and slid them over the side of the bed and sat up. He turned his head until he was looking at the locked door. Or was it locked???? He strained so hard to hear the sound that his body was gradually leaning toward the door. Fearfully he raised his eyes to look through the small window in the door. He sighed audibly, shocked at the unexpected sound. All was dark and shadowless in the hallway. All was normal. Then the sound once again pierced his ears. It chilled him. Why was he so frightened? It didn't make sense. The sound must be real. It couldn't be his imagination. He was safe. There couldn't be anything to fear. And anyway, the door was locked. Locked? He stared at the door. An unbelievable chill, deep within his body, making him shiver. Locked? What could he do if it was open? Where could he hide? There was no place in the small room he could hide, nothing to crouch behind. Just the bed and a small stainless steel stand next to it. If it wasn't locked he could shove it open, look away from the sound and run . . . Where??? Where? Where was he???? Didn't matter. Couldn't go out there anyway. He shook his head. He knew he couldn't go out there. He had no idea what was out there in the darkness . . . in the darkness with the sound. He shivered again. He must get to the door and try to see what was out there . . . Goddam that light! The way it flickered he couldn't be sure the door was closed. He had to find out if it was locked! He lifted his head slightly and leaned further toward the door. No – no, there was no sound. How long had it been since the last time he heard it??? He had no idea. He tried to think about time. He floundered and quickly abandoned the attempt. Then he realized he had no idea what day it was. Month? O God. It's October, isn't it? Yeah. That's right. It's October. Yeah, I'm sure of that. It must be – never ceasing to stare at the door and small window. But it's been so long since the last time he had heard the sound. Too long? Was it outside his door waiting for him? It? It what? It was nothing. Why should anyone . . . anything . . . be out there in the dark waiting for him? O God. Please. Please – a whimpering sound coming from a clenched mouth. The fear that there might be something beyond the door was stronger than the fear that kept him on the side of the bed and forced him to silently slide off and stand leaning against it, his eyes never leaving the door. A spasm jerked his body and thrust him forward. He padded, barefoot and silent, to the door. He stopped abruptly just a foot away. He stared. It must be. It has to be. He closed his eyes. O God – O God! G O D!! With his eyes still closed he thrust his arms forward. The sound of the door banging against the lock broke the silence like the clanging of a steeple bell. He eyes popped open and he stared at the door for a moment, fully assimilating the meaning of the sound. He almost collapsed as his tensed body suddenly relaxed with the realization that the door was locked. *Locked*! He was safe. Safe. Thank God – startled by the sudden sound of his voice. Then his face slowly relaxed into a smile . . . then a frown. Safe from what? Who? He shrugged. What difference does it make now? The door was locked. He was safe. But what was the sound he had heard? How long ago was it now? Had an hour passed? Or was it only minutes? O well, it didn't make any difference now. He smiled securely as he pushed the door, lightly at first, then harder. Securely locked. And nothing . . . no one . . . could break down that door. And anyway, what . . . or who – could be out there? Not important now. His room was impenetrable. He looked through the window but could only see about 10 feet down the narrow and darkened corridor. He put his face against the glass, his face filling the small recess. He shielded his eyes with his hands. Soon he could make out the shapes of the dirty linen baskets against the opposite wall and then the signs above them. He strained his eyes yet could see nothing else. Nothing. He turned his head and looked down the wide, main hallway running perpendicular to the corridor. Nothing. No one . . . His head jerked around as he once more heard the sound. It seemed louder this time. Was it closer? Was that why it was louder? Or was it simply because he was closer to the source? Or was it closer to him? The door? The old, undeniable fear returned. Then slowly the terror subsided. Whatever else might be, he knew the door was locked. That was the only important thing. He was safe. He stared down the corridor for many endless minutes, a vague thought disturbing him. Suppose they had a key. They could get in. But no one was after him. He didn't have to worry about that. He was – there it was again! He peered harder. Nothing. Was it louder? He wasn't certain. If it was moving up the hallway it was moving slowly. Very slowly. He tried to think what it sounded like, but nothing came to mind. It was just a sound. That was it. Of course. That's all it was. It was only a sound. Nothing to fear. Didn't something have to cause a sound? He shook his head, fighting against the logic of this new idea as it tried to force itself and the consequences upon him. No! No! Again he pushed against the door and felt comforted as it resisted the pressure. He leaned even harder against the glass, eyes still shielded with his hands, trying to see a few more feet, a few more inches down the hallway. Then he leaped back from the door and fell over the end of the bed as the lights suddenly went on. He twisted around and stared at the door. He felt his pajamas stick to his sweaty skin. Then he heard the sounds of voices and footsteps coming from the brightly lighted hallway. Faint light slanted through the window over his bed. He looked around the brightly lighted and shadowless room, then fell back on the bed and slept.

Chow time. Chow time.

His sleep had been dreamless and so deep it took many seconds for him to open his eyes. He heard the sound of the large food trays and pans being banged around in the dining hall.

Chow time. He raised his head and looked into the hallway. His door was open and two other inmates walked past on their way to breakfast. The normal sounds of morning were loud and made him jump from the bed. He staggered slightly as he joined the others on their way to the dining hall. Their voices and laughter weren't loud, but the sound of other voices and the activity around him helped prevent any thought of the previous night from disturbing him.

He joined the others standing in line against the far wall in the dining room. The six seats at each of the three stainless steel tables were occupied. He leaned against the wall as his legs threatened to collapse. He wasn't conscious of what anyone was saying, but the sound of voices and the presence of the others was comforting. It helped keep his mind blank. When a seat was available he was given a tray of food, and as he walked to the table he noticed the coffee spilling over the side of the cup. The few feet to the table seemed endless and he gratefully sat down sighing deeply. The sugar was pushed to him and he automatically poured some in his coffee and cereal. He stirred his coffee staring at his tray for several seconds. Then he noticed bread on the tray of the man opposite him. There was none on his. He looked behind him where the food was handed out and he noticed the bread. He looked at the bread for a few seconds, then started to stand, but sat back down. Somehow it didn't seem to be worth all the trouble of walking the few feet to the bread. He turned back to his coffee cup and choked it with both hands, then lowered his head to it. The coffee spilled over into his eggs, but he managed to drink half of it. He put the cup down and sat up straight. He stared at his shaking hands.

Give it up fellas. Give it up. It's been fun, but it's time to run.

The man opposite him got up and carried his tray over to the garbage can, dumped what was left into it, then put the tray on the small cart. He followed, automatically doing the same, then wandered back to his room.

He stood just inside the door and looked around the room – at the bed, the stainless steel stand next to it, then up at the window over the bed. A small bare room. Nothing unusual, yet, at the same time, nothing familiar. He felt as if he had never been here before. But it was only a short time before that he had left this room. He *had* been in this room before. How long? The thought was vague and rushed through his mind. He glanced at the commode, the wash basin and mirror over it. He looked in the mirror. His face was haggard and bearded. He rubbed his chin with a shaking hand. If he could remember when he shaved last, he might be able to figure approximately what day it was. He tried to think but no matter how hard he tried to force his mind it was useless. A thought would almost start to form, then be quickly smothered by a thick haze. He blinked and continued staring at the mirror.

He turned as the door was closed and locked. He glanced at the door, stared at it quizzically for a moment, then shrugged his shoulders and sat on the side of the bed. He opened the drawer of the bedside stand. It was empty except for a few grains of tobacco. He stared at it a second, then closed it and lay down. He looked at the light on the ceiling, then furtively at the wall. He frowned, nodded his head then sat up and looked at the door and the small window in it, his frown deepening. What was it he should remember? What was it that was stuck in his mind ... that was struggling to make itself known? He shook his head and lay back down. He closed his eyes and drifted through a half sleep. It was a good bed. And a thick comfortable pillow. The covers were up around his neck, his hands clutching the edge. He snuggled into the bed, the comfort of a bed and clean sheets almost forgotten, bringing ancient memories vaguely to mind. His bearded face relaxed into a smile as he felt the cool water of the stream on his feet as he stretched out on the grass, his pole beside him. You will never catch any fish like that son. I know Dad, but I just feel like hanging my feet in the stream. I can always get some fish later. The older man looked at his young son and smiled. Maybe you're right Roy. It is a nice day. He continued to look at his only child with, perhaps, a slight hint of envy as the bright sun seemed to make his son's face and blond hair glow. The stream moved with the smallest of sounds, the slight rustling of the leaves on the trees barely audible. Birds flew to and fro deep within the branches and chirped and sang contentedly as they floated and fluttered from tree to sky and sky to ground. Butterflies hovered over groups of buttercups shining amidst green grass.

The boy let his feet hang still as the cool water flowed over them. The warmth from the sun penetrated deep within him. The father smiled, he too responding to the surroundings – the bright sun and the pleasant sounds of a summer's day. It's nice to just lie in the sun and look at the blue sky. He looked back at the stream and the reflection of sky and trees rippled by the movement of the warter. An image drifted into sight and he looked up as a bird reached the apex of its climb – hesitated – sharply defined against the cloudless sky, then banked to the left, glided a few feet, then beat its wings and flew from the man's sight. He looked back at his line where it angled into the water.

The ground felt soft and warm to the boy as he looked straight up, not really conscious of the sky, but vaguely aware of the smell of the earth and grass, hearing the sounds that floated pleasantly through the air. He wiggled his toes and put a blade of grass between his teeth. Maybe in a little while he'd fish. Maybe.

The clanging of the lock dragged him from his reverie. Come and get your medication, Mr. Rawls. Huh? — What? Your medication. Here, extending the small paper cup. He got up abruptly and stepped quickly to the door. She emptied the cup into his hand. Go ahead and take them. He filled a cup with water then swallowed the pills. He looked at her quizzically as she started to close the door. Aaa, how long have I been here? Do you feel alright Mr. Rawls? He thought for a second. I think so. A little shaky. Well the medication will help. He nodded his head and went back to bed as the door was once again locked. He plopped on the side of the bed, then jerked his head toward the door and started to speak. His mouth remained open for a moment, a deep frown on his face, then he shrugged and lay back down on the bed.

He stared at the ceiling, blinking his eyes, then felt something in the pocket of his pajamas as he scratched his shoulder. It was a brown envelope He opened it and took out a yellow form. The first thing he noticed were the words *COUNTY JAIL*. He gazed at it for a moment, then looked up, his eyes half closed as he tried to think ... There were many small boxes on the form with printed titles at the top and handwritten numbers and words in them. He stared for many minutes at the box: *DATE BOOKED*. The date was clear. There was no mistaking it, but what was today's date? If he knew that he would know how long he had been here. He continued to stare at the date thinking as hard as he could, then suddenly, as realization penetrated his mind, started counting on his fingers. So that's what month it is. And it's almost over. Again he forced his memory, trying to recall what month he could last remember. The only thing he was certain of was that it was warm. How many days . . . or months had he forgotten? Trying to remember upset him so he simply let his mind go blank and started to relax. He curled up and drifted through a half slumber until he once again heard the lock clanging and the door opening.

Chow time.

He sat up slowly, then slid from the bed and followed the others to the dining hall.

Automatically falling in line he shuffled along with the others, hearing the sounds of feet, voices and the banging of pans and trays. His tray shook as his cup was filled with coffee. He walked slowly and carefully to the table, but still the coffee spilled over on to the tray. He toyed the food with his spoon then scooped it up and raised it toward his mouth. Halfway up the food fell off the shaking spoon and splattered on the tray. He stared at the empty, wavering spoon, then tried again. He heard faint laughter as he tried again and failed. There seemed to be sound all around him, but he ignored it and concentrated on the elusive food. It was hard, but he did manage to eat some of the food and drink some coffee. By the time he got back to his room he was exhausted and again fell on the bed. There was something he wanted, but it was many minutes before he realized it was a cigarette. He sat up and noticed the door was still open and the other men were slowly walking back to their rooms. He went to the door and asked each man for a smoke, his voice weak, sounding distant. One of the men gave him a cigarette and lit it for him. Feel better today? He half nodded and grunted an answer. You were in bad shape when they brought you in yesterday. *Yesterday*? Looking at him. Don't you remember? He tried to grin. The man smiled. Yeah, that wine can get to you after awhile – *OK. Back to your room.* The man left, and he backed into his room as the door was closed and locked.

He sat on the edge of the bed as he smoked. Been here since yesterday. County Jail. Yeah, that's right, I remember. County Jail. Must have been arrested the night before last if I got up here yesterday. By the time they finish booking you and everything it's a long time. His face flashed into a smile. Yeah. I remember this place. The County Jail Hospital. Self-satisfaction beaming from his face as he congratulated himself for remembering so much. He still couldn't remember being arrested, or where it had occurred. Many months still forgotten, but that knowledge was easily avoided by continuing to think about what he could remember. It was a rare accomplishment lately to remember with such clarity.

Suddenly he looked at the door and strained, for a second, to remember something. But what? The hell with it. Not important. He took a final drag on the cigarette and tossed the butt in the commode.

Once more he luxuriated as he stretched out on the bed. The sun still warm on his face and the water cool on his bared feet. But some clouds drifted through the blue sky and then seemed to fall to earth. Or did a mist rise from the rapidly cooling earth? And what happened to the soothing sounds that had floated through the air, and the gentle breeze that had feathered his face? Then the silence was disturbed with an unfamiliar sound. It seemed to come from the clouds, or somewhere. It couldn't be traced or identified. It was just a sound. Slowly raising himself he lifted his feet from the now silent and cold water, his fishing pole still beside him. He looked toward his father but he seemed to be dissolving in the rapidly increasing mist. He jumped up, wanting to run to Daddy, but he barely moved, his body floating slowly up, then taking many minutes to float to the ground. He called to his father, tears streaming down his cheeks, trying to extend his arms to reach Daddy, but his arms took hours to start to raise and when they did they suddenly were straight down by his sides. Daddy! Daddy! The mist didn't whirl, it was simply there, as was the sound in the air, getting thicker and more impenetrable. The sound didn't get any louder, but it seemed to be more piercing, seeming to remain in his head, increasing and increasing . . .

DADDY!!! An endless screech, the arms still refusing to respond, Daddy becoming vaguer and vaguer ... tears still flowing down his face, panic making breathing difficult ...

A deep agonizing groan dragged him from sleep. He shook his head and sat up, his face slightly stiff from dried tears. He thought hard trying to identify the sound that woke him. Panic spun his head – he looked at the light, the window, the door, vague memories tormenting him, yet never defining themselves. The light burned bright and constant; the corridor outside his door still illuminated. It's ok. Everything's ok. The sound of his voice startled him slightly. The panic subsided, but the vague uneasiness still pervaded him. He sat still, staring at the wall, on the verge of tears ...

The sound of the door being opened forced his head around. Medication, Mr. Rawls. She put the cup of pills on the sink. The door was slammed shut. He stepped over to the sink and picked up the cup. The sound of the pills rattling in the cup brought a frown to his face. He stared at the jumping pills for a moment before he put them in his mouth, filled the cup with water then slowly raised it, lowered his head and drank the water. Turning, he started to go back to the bed, then stopped and put the cup on top of the sink, nodding his head with satisfaction at the cup before going back to the bed.

His preoccupation with the vague feeling that there was something he should remember lasted through dinner and the remainder of the evening. He tried so hard to remember what was on the fringe of his consciousness that it was painful, the effort so enervating that shortly before the lights were turned out he fell into an exhausted sleep.

The sweat prickling his sides and burning his eyes forced him to rub them and shake his head. He turned slightly and fell back against the door, a fearful cry forced from his throat as his reflection leaped at him from the mirror, the staring eyes burning back at him unfamiliar. Many moments passed before he realized that the sound frightening him came from his throat as he fought to get air in his lungs ... the recognition eventually registering as he stared at his image. He tentatively touched the red spot on his forehead, marked by pressing his head against the window in the door. He leaned against the door, vaguely aware of the leaping shadows and the sound from the flickering night light. Then slowly he became aware of where he was. He stared at the empty bed and crumpled linen – then swiftly turned around, his head hitting the door. Quickly he turned around again, again falling against the door. The sound from the stuttering light more frightening than the spastic shadows rolling through the room. The crawling sweat stung, yet he couldn't move his hand to wipe his eyes. Eventually the pain in his chest and the feeling of suffocation forced an end to his paralysis. He deliberately took a few deep breaths until his breathing was almost normal. Many times he looked at the short space between his bed and where he leaned against the door. He felt sure he was leaning against the door – he must be, he had to be – but the only thing he could remember was sitting on the edge of the bed. Maybe he was still there – somehow – yet he could feel the door against his back. He couldn't be sitting on the bed. Slowly he reached back, his eyes closed, and touched the door. He opened his eyes. He looked at the bed. It was empty. He must be standing here leaning against the door. THE DOOR! THE DOOR!

His body jerked spastically. Something was familiar. He whimpered as a battle screamed in his head and something fought to be remembered. He wanted to get back to his bed, pull the sheet over his head and blank the sound and mayhem from his mind, but movement was impossible. He tried leaning forward to force himself to move, but fear continued to paralyze him. If only he could.

ooohhh ... ooohhh, the whimpering cry wrenched pathetically from his twitching mouth. He stumbled around, fell against the wall and slid to the floor never ceasing his whining as he curled in a corner, the shuffling sound still resounding in his head, trying to disappear in the corner as the memory of the previous night suddenly saturated his mind. A blubbering, simpering NO slobbered from his lips. He wanted to dissolve as he pushed harder into the corner; yet, too, he tried desperately to reach to someone unseen for comfort, but his arms remained wrapped tightly around his chest.

He remained huddled in the corner until the sound stopped reverberating in his head. Then all was silent. All was silent save the flickering light. Even his breathing. The distraction of watching the shadows tumble about the room helped calm him, as did the sound clicking from the light. Time was meaningless, non-existent, as his arms slowly loosened from around him and ended up resting on his crossed legs. He sat thus for many minutes . . . . . .

Eventually he raised his head and looked up toward the small window in the door. As terrified as he was of standing and looking through the window, he was more terrified of not knowing what might be out there. He continued to sit in the corner weighing his fears – then his eyes brightened slightly with remembrance. He pushed against the door tentatively – looked at it – shoved it again, harder, then leaned his weight against it as he slowly and fearfully raised himself to his feet and approached the window.

Oh please God, Please. Don't let it be there. It *has* to be silent out there. It just *has* to be. The shadows mottled his face as he got closer and closer to the window, not stopping until his face was pressed hard against the glass. Sweat continued to trickle and the light flickered noisily.

He squeezed his eyes shut tighter and tighter until they ached. He listened . . . listened . . .

the only sounds that of the light and his breathing. His lids slowly separated and he became conscious of the gloom of the darkened corridor. Soon his eyes were accustomed to the darkness and familiar objects and the silence eased some of the tension in his body. Maybe he hadn't heard it. Heard what? If he had, what did it sound like? If he couldn't remember anything about the sound then maybe it didn't exist. The empty bed was reflected in the window. It's still empty so he must be leaning against the door. Yeah, he was here looking through the window trying to see down the corridor. But that doesn't mean there's a sound out there. No matter how real this is, it doesn't mean it's out there. But what was he doing here?

He knew he had been in the bed. Of this he was certain. Of course he was. Just look at the way the linen was all messed up. Yeah, it's only a few feet, a few steps, from the side of the bed to the door, but that doesn't mean anything either.

But how – Uhhh – Pain shocked him as the sound once again reached his ears and his body stiffened. Then all was silent. Not even the clicking of the light could be heard. Holding his breath he remained pressed against the door, conscious of nothing, not even the pain in his stiffened body. He listened intently, his body starting to twitch. His vision blurred as his head vibrated violently. His muscles cramped so painfully that he instinctively forced his body to relax before it shattered from the tension.

Then it came again, a little louder. And a little closer? It seemed to be. His body trembled as he tried to figure just how close it was. Or how far away. Yes. Away. He would think of it as far away. But that would mean it was huge if it was far away and he could still hear it so plainly. No matter how he thought of it, he could find no comfort. His whimpering was louder than the flickering light.

He stood petrified against the door. Again time was suspended until it was moved by the sound piercing the dark silence. Tears dropped from his eyes and he clutched at the door. This time there was no doubt about its being louder. And too he started to recognize it, but he fought desperately against this recognition. His head was shaking as he continued to fight and blubber. He tried to speak, but only an incoherent groan was agonizingly wrenched from his throat.

The glass in the window was wet with his tears as the sound shuffled closer and louder, his pleading increasing in intensity and volume in his mind, only a wet blubbering coming from his mouth.

His arms were stretched above him, his hands still tapping pathetically against the door as he slowly, still whimpering, folded to the floor, slowly stretching out on his back as tears rolled down his cheeks, spittle dribbling from his mouth. He fell into the release of unconsciousness.

Light stabbed his eyes and he moved slightly and smiled for a moment. Then he frowned as the sun failed to warm him. And why was the ground so hard and bare of grass? And the sounds that should be floating through the air were missing. The silence was startling.

He opened his eyes, then closed them immediately as they focused on the ceiling light. He turned his head and opened his eyes again. His vision was filled with the grayness of the door. He looked up and saw the sink. He could feel the coolness of the concrete floor and understanding slowly seeped into his mind. He sat up, hesitated for a second as he looked at the bed, then stood up. He looked all around the room – once, twice, then satisfied he sat on the edge of the bed. He shook his head . . . shook it again, harder, as if shaking off a blow. Yeah, this was his room. He remembered it. Yet something was wrong. But what? He remembered being in the room and it hadn't changed. But he had been on the floor . . .

The hell with it. He had awakened so many times in unfamiliar places with no memory of how he had gotten there that he just shook it off. Yet he felt something was different this time. What in the hell was it that kept nagging at him???? It couldn't be anything. He was in a locked room and he wasn't drunk. No, there couldn't be anything wrong. He went to the sink and splashed cold water on his face. He wiped at his face with a towel, then sat back on the edge of the bed until the door was opened and he went to the dining room.

All through the day he responded automatically and un-questioningly to the calls for medication and food. In between he sat on his bed still feeling uneasy about something. Usually his mind was blank, or at least he couldn't remember thinking about anything. But now there was something bothering him. O hell, it's nothing. Better to concentrate on the goddamn itch that was bugging him. He looked at the red streaks and blotches on his hands and arms. He looked at his legs covered with the same angry red streaks. He examined them carefully. Ain't a damn bug anywhere. The sound of his voice startled him for a second, but he simply shrugged and continued speaking aloud, as if he were talking to someone sitting opposite him. Again and again he tried to find the lice that he knew were crawling all over him, always without success. He scratched – hands, arms, chest, every part of his body he could reach. He scratched so hard he drew blood from the back of his hand. What the hell is that? The sons of bitches bit me so hard I'm bleeding – looking at the small drop of blood. Ain't never had nothing like this before. Can't even see the bastards. Go ahead you bastards, crawl your asses off. I don't give a good goddamn. And what the hell you laughing at you lousy bastard? Yeah, that's it. You better leave I dont need any of your shit. At least I know what a clean bed is. That's more than you can say ... Oh bullshit. Go on. Get the hell out of here – waving his arm. Wise ass. It's just an itch. That's all. Just a damn itch – scratching and scratching, the back of one hand smeared with blood. He rubbed his face with both hands, pressing hard on his burning eyes, and shook his head.

He lay down, frowning for a moment, thinking, but nothing defined itself so he let his face relax and closed his eyes. He continued scratching as he drifted toward oblivion. He tossed and mumbled as an image started to form in the mist over his head. The features weren't distinct, but he was aware of a full thick beard and felt accusation burning into him. The image started to become more distinct as he gradually penetrated the fringe of unconsciousness. He mumbled louder and struggled back and forth on the bed as he fought the accusing eyes of the image. He screamed again and again, the sound of his terrified voice loud in his head, but no sound passed his lips. He continued to fling his body from side to side, his screaming voice continuing to pierce his mind, until he hit the corner of the bedstand, hard, with the back of his hand, the pain quickly yanking him awake. His breathing was rapid and shallow as he waited for the fear to drain from him.

After many minutes he became aware of the pain in his hand and sat up and started rubbing it. Soon, he didn't know when, he stopped rubbing and was scratching. Later he was still trembling, unaware that he was scratching all over with both hands. There was no attempt at thought, remembering or understanding. Only the sound of his pleading voice preventing a complete collapse. Was it sweat or tears that moistened his face? Or both? He covered his face with his hands, then looked at his moist palms. I don't know why it's raining. Every time I want to do something it rains, the rain suddenly turning into a downpour and roaring from the heavens drowning his screams. He watched as the young boy ran from the brook into the trees. He heard nothing as he ran and stumbled toward the swaying trees. He felt his pounding heart and saw his father vaguely through the cascade of rain, his arms waving and yelling to the fleeing boy to stay away. He continued to run through the trees, then suddenly seemed suspended as lightning cracked and flashed, a huge oak splitting and groaning to the ground, his father disappearing in the fiery flash and smoke.

He rocked back and forth on the side of the bed, face covered with reddened hands, trying to whine away the image. He lowered his hands, still rocking, and stared at the wall until he saw the floating shadows and the sound of rain and lightning faded away. He scratched harder and harder. It's just that my skin's dry, you stupid son of a bitch. I ain't got no damn bugs. And anyway it's none of your damn business. Get lost. He nodded at the wall. He's nothing but a big mouth. I'm not afraid of the rain. I'm not afraid of nothing. You just watch. I'll show them. And anyway, I don't care. Let them say what they want. I don't care. The back of both hands were seeping blood, his head continually nodding, as he rambled on. What do you want . . . the shadows suddenly started sliding down the wall as the lights went out and the night light flickered. He watched the shadows and faint splotches of light floating from one form into another. He scratched a thigh with one hand, a cheek with the other. Ha – hehehe –hahahahaha – Yeah. That's it. Go getim.

HA HA HA HA HA HA

His laugh dissolved into a giggle as Mickey Mouse butted Donald Duck with his antlers. Then Donald fell to the floor and jumped on a motorcycle and roared under the bed. Mickey leaped from the wall onto his motorcycle, but it wouldn't start. He leaned over, anxiously watching Mickey kicking the starter. Comeon Mickey, comeon, Hurry up. Getim, Getim, bouncing up and down.

BA ROOOMMM

ROORMMMM

BRRUPPPPP

UPPPP

A ROOMMMMM

That's it Mickey. He's under the bed, getim, getim. Mickey roared off with a screech of burning tires. He leaned all the way over, clapping his hands as Mickey disappeared under the bed. Then Donald roared out from under the end of the bed and leaned into a sharp turn, just missing the door. Mickey quickly followed. They raced around the room, under the bedstand, the bed, up one wall, down another, and across the ceiling. He fell back on the bed, twisting in all directions as he watched the pursuit with bouncing glee.

Abruptly there was silence as they disappeared under the bed. He leaned over and waited for a few minutes, then slid off the bed, kneeled on the floor and looked under it. Come out. Come on fellas. Come on out. He stared into the corner, then slowly scanned the entire area, reaching under the bed as he flattened himself on his stomach. Where are you? What happened, Mickey? Why did you stop? We were having fun. Please come . . . he froze, his body rigid as he lay motionless on the floor, his head and arms under the bed listening . . . listening . . .

then he scrambled under the bed as the sound once again shattered the stillness. He huddled under the bed, his nails digging into the palms of his hands. A low wail bubbled in his throat as the sound shuffled closer and closer . . . louder and louder. He rolled on the floor trying to compress himself into an invisible ball and disappear into the wall. He scrambled so desperately that he banged his head into the wall again and again and crashed into the underside of the bed, the sound shuffling closer and closer.

Then he heard it. Distinctly. And everything suddenly started strangling him: the previous nights; the dreams; the warm sun and cool brook; the song of birds and gentle breezes; the sudden stinging of the flooding rain, the lightning and the groaning splitting of the tree and the gagging smell of smoke. It all descended on him as the sound threatened to crush the door. And with it a new sound, a pelting sound of rain falling on leafy trees.

The bed bounced wildly as he continued to scramble until he once more froze and just screamed, then suddenly bolted up, the bed falling over on its side, as the sound was no longer one of rain on leaves, but that of dirt falling on a wooden box. His piercing screams grew louder and echoed through the corridors . . .

The orderlies and nurse rushed to his room and looked through the window, then quickly opened the door.

His screeching became louder as he saw the sound peering at him through the window. He curled into the corner behind the overturned bed, tears streaming from his eyes as the door opened and the sound started in.

They stood looking at him for a moment, then one of the orderlies rushed away, returning quickly with a restraining sheet.

His feet scratched madly against the floor as he once more screeched hysterically and cringed into the wall as the sound came toward him, partially hidden by a white mist . . .

Then it was silent. Its work accomplished.

Im Being Good

Dear Harold:

we get pills 4 times a day and it makes me very drowsy. I am having trouble writing. we have to stay awake all day and its hard. my eyes hurt all the time. I dont know how long exactly Ive been here but they dont let you lay down during the day. the place is locked where they keep the beds. Its all sort of like a big long room with small rooms. they get us up early in the morning. the trees are bare and there are lots of birds I can see them from the window. they almost look like funny leaves.they make a lot of noise bird noise. I think I saw a doctor sometimes but I dont know. he talked funny. the birds are very noisy I think before daylight they make a lot of noise. when they wake us up a woman comes and yells and I worry the sun wont come up. Im so tired. the sun will come up wont it harold?

Jan. 10

Dear Harold:

I dont think Im so confused today. I wish I didnt have to take the medicine it makes me so tired I feel so sick in my stomach all the time. O I wish I could sleep for a long time. but Im not hungry. but sometimes a little bit I feel like eating but I cant chew it hurts my jaws or something to chew. they ache and the ears. I cant seem to hear so good. was I hearing good when you visited? I hope I was hearing good and heard you and the children together. they looked so nice in their dresses and roberts new clothes. I hope they get nice things for christmas. they could use some clothes. O it makes me sad they dont have new clothes. I mean brand new clothes for the holidays. but we had a nice visit. but I miss everyone. I wish the children could come and see me. but they wont let them why wont they let them visit me? Im their mother I know I am. they look like me dont they? they call me mommy. but we had a nice talk didnt we harold? it was a nice visit and we talked. and you looked so nice. and I liked the candy bars you brought I think I ate them all already. O harold you did visit? I know my eyes hurt so much and Im so tired but you did visit didnt you harold? didnt you please.

Jan. 12

Dear Harold:
I feel very cold. the birds were so loud today they chased the sun away. its still dark so dark I can feel it in my stomach. and in my bones its so cold because the sun didnt come up. I wish it would come up and be warm. I dont like it so cold.

Jan. 16

Dear Harold:
We cant sleep during the day. theres no chairs. I sneaked into a corner and I think I sleeped but they caught me and made me get up. you see theres lots of us in the room. Its big and has some great big wooden benches. you cant pick them up or even hardly move them I dont think. They let us out sometimes to go pee pee but I dont think some people go there. we are in this room all day. I think they play music. Theres a couple of girls they walk around

all day. I think Ive been in this room before. I dont think this is the first day. Maybe for lots of days. I dont know they dont tell me but its warmer today. and the birds were noisy this morning very noisy but its warmer anyway. Why is that harold? how come its warm and theres day light when the birds screamed this morning? I think they scream every morning. its so terrible its like a million zillion monkeys or little babys making funny noises only its not the same but every morning when its still dark they make a terrible racket and then this woman comes around and screams to get up and sometimes bangs the bed. but we dont have to walk far to the eating place its just outside. I think and the showers too sometimes. I can get by the window for a while and I see people walking around outside. it looks cold.

Jan. 26

Dear Harold:

Im pretty sure Ive written other letters. I cant seem to remember too well. I think I have some from you which I read today. but I dont seem to remember them but Im glad you wrote. I dont remember the holidays but I hope the children had fun and liked the tree and santa. I wonder how come I dont remember the holidays? I guess maybe I was in here I dont think I know how long. I think they said I came here the day before the day before christmas eve. I know it was something about christmas or christmas eve but I cant remember if it was christmas eve or the day before. O Harold I didnt want to miss christmas eve again I really didnt. I wanted to be home I honestly to goodness did want to be home with my family with you on christmas eve so we could fill the stockings and put up the tree and put the presents around. and the lights I love the lights on the tree with the big white angel on top and the blue light under it. O remember how Bobby clapped his hands the first time he saw the angel. he thought it flew to the top of the tree and wanted it to fly down. and he waited and waited and Im sorry harold please forgive me for not being home on christmas eve. how are the children? are they alright? did they have a good christmas? did the gramas and granpas make big over them? I hope it was a good christmas. did you eat lots of nice pies and stuff. I hope the children had a good time. are they alright? O Harold I wish you would write. how are you?

Jan. 28

Dear Harold:

There are so many of us in this room. Have you seen it! when you were here? I dont think so I think they dont have visitors here only in the visiting room where you sit with your visitors. there are a lot of us in the room and some of them are so angry and growl and sometimes hit. I think maybe some of them are bad. but Im being good. the attendants call them bad and take them out someplace and sometimes they scream but I guess youve never seen this room. theres a window on the door. its always locked. we are put in here right after breakfast except if we have a shower and sometimes we can brush our hair. sometimes I get up early enough to brush my hair. the birds are always making noises before sunrise. its an awful racket and sometimes I get up before the attendant comes and screams to get up and brush my hair. at least I know I did it this morning. they dont let you have a comb but I dont like one anyway. I think maybe Ive gotten up a couple of times and brushed my hair before breakfast. Im trying to eat like they tell me so I can get some strength and go home. Im sorry I missed the holiday but they said if I eat and get strong I can go home and even if I wasnt home for christmas eve and the holidays. I could maybe be alright to go home for easter. If not for good maybe at least anyway on a pass. I wish I wasnt here. I dont like it here. Im scared. I wish I was home. I think its the pills that make me so tired. Im being good. its different ones now. theyre green. Im not so tired but sometimes I just wish I could lie down and take a nap even just a little nap. its so hard to move I can hardly lift my feet sometimes. I just sort of shuffle and these funny slippers they give us keep coming off. O how are the children? I miss them so much. I wish they didnt run around so much. I hope mother doesnt let them run around so much back and forth all day. tell them I miss them and give them a big kiss from me and make sure theyre quiet. they wont bother you to get upset.

Feb.4

Dear Harold:

There was a terrible big fight here last nite. after they opened the doors to the dormitory where we sleep. they open them I think about 8 oclock and you can go to bed after night time pills. one of the women walks around the room all day, the room we're locked in all day, and growls and swears and they dont seem to growl at anyone but just sort of to themselves. they frighten me. I wish they were somewhere else. I try and watch them all day so they cant hurt me but sometimes Im so sleepy I cant keep my eye on them. and sometimes they just scream out loud and slap the air like windmills or maybe its not all of them but only the one, the one I was telling you about who started the big fight. she suddenly grabbed another woman and accused her of taking her sunday shoes and started to strangle her and the woman started hitting her and we all screamed and some of them started pounding on the door but they wouldnt open the door and it was really terrible and I was scared to death but I was good. and the woman kept choking her and finally the attendants came in and grabbed the women and dragged her away but the strangling lady wouldnt stop screaming about her sunday shoes and she starting hitting the attendants. and so the attendants dragged her into a room and kept her there for awhile and there was an awful commotion and when they brought her out she was in a straightjacket and couldnt stand and they dragged her down the hall but they wouldnt let us watch. they put us all back in the

IM BEING GOOD   113

room and locked the door. I didnt see her today. a lady whispered to me that they put her in a dungeon way way down under the building. I dont think I believe that.

Feb. 10

Dear Harold:

They let me watch television for a while last night. It was nice. its a nice room with regular chairs. you know, lounge chairs and those other plastic ones. I sat in a plastic chair, but if I get to the t.v. room earlier I might be able to get a regular sitting chair. it was kind of relaxing. I mean everyone seemed to be quiet and some of the ladies were sleeping. mostly the ones in the easy chairs. it didnt seem fair that they took up the really good chairs and slept. I wish they would let them go to bed and then maybe I could have one of those chairs but maybe if I get there earlier tonight. theyre going to let me go every night. most of the people there are from the open wards. were in what they call the locked ward because were locked in all day. theres only 3 of us allowed from the locked ward. were being good. the people on the open wards have a lot of places they can walk around. I think they can even go outside but its cold now. theres a canteen where you can get things and they can go there. I think they also have a movie sometimes and other things. a library too. maybe if I keep being good theyll put me on an open ward and I can get one of those nice big easy chairs to sit in. during the day too. how are you?

Feb. 15

Dear Harold:

It was a nice visit. thank you for coming on Valentines Day. you look so handsome in your suit. and thats my favorite tie. Im so glad you wore it. I was really sorry when the visiting time was over. its always so sad to see all those people walking down the path to the cars and buses. we stay by the window when they let us and watch the visitors go. sometimes we stay there a long time afterwards. they tell us its not good to do that. that we upset ourselves but its so hard to leave the window even after theres nobody there anymore. I watched a candy wrapper blow down the walk and across the street. I watched it all the way to the fence. I couldnt see if it went through the fence. Im still allowed to go to the open ward at night. now right after supper. we sit in the chairs and talk or just sit. I like the television too. there was some funny programs on last night. we laughed a lot. at least some of us did. I guess its not such a loud laugh but we do laugh. sometimes some ladies just sleep. I dont seem to be as sleepy as I was. Im only getting 2 little pills a day now. I hope you can visit soon. I miss you. its been so long since Ive seen you. I know its hard with kids yelling and screaming and running around. maybe in a bigger place. they wont upset you. are you feeling better?

Feb. 20

Dear Harold:

I was going to wait until your visit to tell you the good news but I cant wait so Im writing. theyre letting me out on the open ward during the day. I still have to come back here to the locked ward to sleep but during the day I can stay on the open ward. its sort of a trial basis and if Im good it will become permanent. isnt that wonderful? Im really excited. today was my first day. I walked around and its so nice. nobody was growling or screaming like those other ladies and there are chairs to sit in and books to read if you can stay awake. they have jigsaw puzzles too. And you can go to the bathroom any time you want to. anytime. and I am going to go to occupational therapy too. I promise not to make any more wallets or book marks, maybe just a new belt for Bobby. I know O.T. doesnt seem like much but its something to do to break the boredom. it gets so tedious. but they have something new theyre going to try starting next week. its some kind of writing class. I dont know what kind of writing but theyll provide all the supplies. I think Im getting better. I hope easter hurries up and gets here. maybe you can come see me soon.

Feb. 27

Dear Harold:

It seems like so long since Ive written. has it been? I havent kept track. I am looking forward to your visit. it will be good to hold hands though I must confess I feel embarrassed in the visiting room. youll look so sexy in your 3 piece suit and my favorite tie. and just like I promised Im doing everything they tell me and being real good. Im sure theyll let me home for easter maybe for a couple of days. Im really feeling stronger and stronger each day. I cant wait to see my little darlings and give them all a big hug and kiss. thousands of them. like I promised Im not doing any leather work. just needlepoint. and its not a home sweet home. its a nice picture of a kitten and a ball. youll like it when its finished. we can always give it to your mother for christmas.

The writing class, its called OT-III-writing, is kind of fun. its co-ed and there was a lot of moving around as the men tried to get to sit near the pretty girls, and some of the girls did some moving around too. it looked like there was going to be fooling around all day for a while, but the woman leading the class got things under control fast enough. theres only about a dozen of us so its not too bad. some people read a few things and then we talked about writing something during the week and then reading it at the next class. I thought I'd write something about ice cream cones. I know it sounds silly but it might be fun. you know when you were a kid how you had to push the ice cream down right away without breaking the cone, and then how you had to lick the edges and be careful how you bit the cone. and how you kissed it up to God if you dropped it on the ground before you started eating it again, no matter how dirty it got. I think its a fun idea. What do you think? anyway, it gives me something to think about for the next week. how are you? I no I'll be seeing you soon.

March 7

Dear Harold:

I've been spending most of my time writing that piece about ice cream cones I mentioned to you. its so much fun. it brought back a lot of memories about my childhood and especially the summer time and the times we all went to the beach and Coney Island and the rides. it was a marvelous time of my life. so happy and carefree. nothing to do but run around and play games. we used to go to the park a lot when we were kids. you couldn't get a real ice cream cone there, but there was always an ice cream truck of some kind, usually a good humor. I remember there was always a breeze on the top of the hill, and I used to love the feel of the air on my face as I ran down the hill screaming and screeching. kids love to scream and screech dont they. but I was a good girl, I really was. I was quiet.

We had a good time at the writing class this week. we got down to work much faster this week and there was less maneuvering. It looked like a couple of them were playing a little more then kneesees in the back of the room. some people had written some things and read them and they were nice. one girl wrote a real nice poem and she let me copy it. Here it is.

I walk along a quiet shore,
And look at the ocean still,
Whilst thinking of the one I adore,
And wondering does he love me still.

I close my eyes and kiss his hand,
And bathe in the light of his eyes,
And sink my feet into the sand
And wonder where does his heart lie.

And then I know where heart and love
Can blend and be soothing and warm,
As I gaze into his face above,
Then surrender into my lovers arms.

Isn't that nice? I guess its not a great poem, but I love it. it has such a nice feeling. we're all so lonely here. I've been really good. you can visit now, can't you?

March 9th

Dear Harold:
   I'm sorry you still cant get to visit. I no the kids bother you and you cant stand them but Im here. no kids. and Im being really good and doing everything Im told. Im sure I can get a pass for easter if you would come get me. probably the whole weekend. we could go some place alone. I could meet you. where would you like to go? I dont care. if we could just be together. I miss you so much. it seems like forever since I saw you. I wish you would hold me and everything. lots of fathers get upset by their kids. Ill make sure they wont bother you. we wont see them. just the two of us for the whole weekend. we could be happy. if you could just write. O I hope easter comes early this year.

Mar 14

Dear Harold:
   Im in the writing class and cant stop crying and Im afraid to let them see me or theyll put me back in the locked ward and I dont want to go back there I cant let them see me cry but I cant seem to stop. I want so much to see you I miss you so much and the doctor said I shouldnt go home for easter but should wait a while maybe next month when the weathers nicer and I was looking forward to being with you and snuggling in your arms and

everything but now they wont let me out even for a day and if they see me crying I just know theyll put me back in that ward. O I wish you could come see me or write or something now instead of worrying about those little monsters whore always interfering in everything O just let us be alone for a second and no matter where they are it could be a hundred miles and they would no it and come running to make sure we dont have any time together. O I know they chased you away but what about my attention? I cant get out to even take a walk and you cant come to visit. and in the writing class when I started to read my peace I only got to read about a page when one of the men started yelling and screaming at me that I had no right to write such silliness when children all over the world were starving and dying like flies and all kinds of horrible things he said to me and accused me as if I were some sort of monster and Im trying to be so good I honestly am Im even eating all the food. I love my children honest honest true I love them and dont want them to go to a home or some place O I wish I could stop crying. I dont want them to see me crying so Im trying to write something for the class pretty soon itll be dark in the tv room and no one will see my eyes I cant let them know Ive been crying O harold please where are you please

SYLVIA WILSON   O.T.-III WRITING

MY RETURN TO LOWELL STATE HOSPITAL

I had spent 7 months here between 1978 and 1979. when I left I said I hope I would never have to return again, not knowing that god has ways that we become sick to the point that only hospital care would be the only way out. In august of this year my children and myself were living in Sheepshead bay on welfare. I was told to go to court because my husband was back on payments toward our support. not that this has anything to do with this but it seemed that my voices started with a court house. one week after going there I started to hear voices that seemed to be having a large court session on all the past friends and people that I had known from a little girl. hearing their voices and debating on putting me in a institution, for things that I was falsely being accused of. these voices continued night and day for about three weeks and then it ceased. then there was a group of men and women who said they were a hired mind readers organization speaking to me mental telepathy and had picked my mind up on the beach. they were telling me we had only until xmas to live and to either commit suicide or they will come up on xmas eve in santa clause uniforms and kill us. so through the strain of it all for my childrens sake I gave up and came willingly back to lowell state hospital for my cure. the voices remained with me for 2 or 3 weeks and then they just politely walked out of my life. the peace and quiet is wonderful. I hope they dont come back. O please dont come back.

Indian Summer

The sky was cloudless and blue, the air warm, crisply clear. The previous few days had been prematurely cool, but today was the kind of day you dream of all through a hot humid summer of stifling subways, burning pavements and faulty air conditioners. And it was Sunday. He could just sit around and read the Times and later watch the Jets game.

Yes, a truly marvelous day. And for New York a rare one. You dont get too many days like this where the air is so clear and clean you feel as if you could rub it between your finger tips. He breathed deeply as he left the newsstand with his Times, and stopped for a moment to enjoy the sky and the relaxed quiet of the morning, thinking of the day of leisure that awaited him.

He glanced at the newspaper and smiled as he anticipated sitting in their small backyard and going through the many bulky sections, looking forward with eagerness to reading the sports pages now that the football season had begun. And too, an occasional can of cold beer wouldnt dim his spirits any. He breathed deeply again and smiled as he looked up and down the tree-lined street. It sure will be good to relax after the hectic week he just put in. That damn Goodwin account is enough to drive anyone batty. But he wasnt going to think about that now. Not on a day like this. Thats how you get ulcers. No, he was just going to relax and take it easy and leave that for tomorrow. Monday morning will come soon enough. It always does.

I wonder if we should go for a drive? The countryside will be lovely with the trees changing colors and the fall flowers blooming. Bet it would be beautiful in Connecticut, and we could stop at a nice restaurant and have dinner. Im sure Ethel would like that. Give her a chance to get out of the kitchen, and Suzie likes riding in the car – bouncing the Times against his hip as he walked – but the damn road will be packed with Sunday drivers and we would probably hit one traffic jam after another. No, I guess it would be better to just forget the whole thing and spend a nice quiet day at home. Actually Sunday is really a day to spend at home with the family, and he did not want to miss the Jets game, hoping Ethel would not say anything about being a football widow.

When he got home his wife was just finishing the breakfast dishes. He put an arm around her waist as he kissed her on the cheek. Its a beautiful day.

Yes, I know. I was out back for a few minutes before. Makes you feel like doing something or going somewhere.

Yeah, I suppose it does, but what it really makes me want to do is sit in the sun with the Times and a beer. After all, I have to be well rested if Im going to do a good job at the office. He smiled at his wife and kissed her again, then put the paper on the table and took a can of beer out of the refrigerator. Wheres Suzie?

In her room.

O. Shes so quiet I thought maybe she was in the yard.

No. Shes playing with her coloring book. Ethel dried her hands and hung up the towel. You know Harry, it might be a good idea if you took Suzie to the park later. Maybe while Im fixing dinner you can take her to the playground.

Gee, I dont know honey. I was planning on taking it easy today. I put in a rough week and I have another one in front of me.

I know, darling, but it would be nice if you could.

Well, we/ll see what happens.

He started to go out to the yard when Suzie came out of her room. We going to the park, daddy?

Maybe later, sweetheart – patting her on the head.

On the swings?

We/ll see, honey. Maybe later. Right now daddy has

something to do – still patting her on the head – maybe in a little while. Suzie looked up at him for a moment then went back to her room.

Harry went out into the yard and moved his chair so it was in the sun and started reading the paper. Whether or not he took Suzie to the playground wasnt a matter of life or death. She did look a little disappointed, but it wasnt that important. And that damn Goodwin account. And anyway, its still early. He could always take her later, after he read at least part of the paper and relaxed for a while. There/d be time before dinner. Perhaps he should spend a little more time with her alone. He really didnt spend too much time with her and lately she was almost ready for bed by the time he got home. Of course that wasnt his fault, but still . . . when was the last time he took her to the park? Well, after all thats not really my responsibilty. Harry continued reading, vaguely aware of the sound of voices coming from the house.

He glanced up at the sky from time to time and breathed deeply. He browsed through the "News of the Week in Review" section noting a few headlines, looking at all the political cartoons and reading their captions. Harry slowly leafed through the Theater Section and decided to save the Magazine and Book Review Section for after dinner, before the game. Keeping the Sports Section on his lap he put the remainder of the paper on the ground then stretched his legs and leaned back in his chair.

The sun was warm on Harry Swansons face as it slowly rose higher in the sky, moving from his left to his right. He finished the beer and thought for a moment about getting another, but the idea gradually faded as he continued reading. When he finished reading about all the games he thumbed through the rest of the section, then let the paper slide from his hand and had one last cigarette before going back into the house.

He plopped the paper on the couch and stretched his arms out over his head a few times while rocking back and forth on the balls of his feet. Man O man, what a beautiful day. Its really beautiful out Ethel, you should go out and enjoy it and do whatever youre doing later.

I think I will, in just a few minutes, as soon as I get the roast started.

Suzie still coloring?

I dont know. I suppose so. Shes being quiet so Im not going to look at any gift horses.

Harry smiled, I know what you mean. He put his hands in his pockets and rocked on the balls of his feet, I was thinking maybe I/d take her to the park before dinner. Itll be a couple of hours yet, wont it?

Thats a good idea. Figure about 2:30, or maybe youd better make it 2 to be on the safe side.

O.K. You want to get her ready?

Suzie had learned how to skip and she tugged Harrys arms as she periodically started skipping. Harry asked her several times to stop, yanking her arm once to emphasize his request but she could not stop using her new toy so Harry eventually let go of her hand cautioning her not to cross the street without him. When they got to the park Suzie started running toward the playground, but Harry stopped her. Wait a minute honey, daddy wants to go over there for a few minutes first.

A crowd of a few hundred people were watching a football game and Harry, holding Suzies hand, walked to the near side of the field and rapidly worked his way to the sideline, pushing Suzie in front of him. Between plays he questioned those around him until he learned the score and the quarter and how the game was going.

Harry immediately became involved in the game and impatiently told Suzie to wait a minute, just a few more minutes, as she pulled at his arm. Swings daddy, I want the swings – and she wriggled and squirmed between the many sets of legs surrounding her as the crowd moved with the development of each play.

Eventually Harry became aware of Suzies petulance and picked her up and held her so her head was on a level with his.

There we are, honey. Is that better?

My nose itches.

Well rub it, honey.

Can we go on the swings now?

Just a few minutes and they/ll stop, then we/ll go. I promise. Harry continued to watch each play unfold, ooing and aaing with the crowd and, of course, quarterbacking; and Suzie continued to ask to go to the swings and squirm with boredom, and Harry growing more and more impatient with her insistence telling her to stop and stay still and squeezing her thigh a few times to emphasize his demand.

When the half finally ended Harry wanted to talk to the others about the game, but Suzie wiggled around so much he knew it would be useless to try so he left the crowd of spectators and put Suzie down. O.K., o.k., we/ll go to the playground. You happy now? completely exasperated and frustrated. She trotted off, her mind empty of everything but the forthcoming pleasure of the swings, the sliding pond and the see-saw, Harry walking rapidly behind her, turning his head occasionally to look back at the football field.

Suzie was hanging from a swing when Harry caught up with her. Now be careful. Youll hurt yourself doing that. He picked her up and put her in the swing and told her to hold on tightly to the safety bar across the front. He pushed the swing and Suzie kicked her legs with glee and at first Harry told her to stop kicking and to sit still, but after a few minutes of his daughters giggling, and the silence from the football field, he relaxed and continued pushing until Suzie suddenly announced, Sliding pond.

He held his hands out ready to catch her as she climbed the steps one by one, then waited for her at the end of the slide, but she vigorously shook her head, no, and so he allowed her to slide down alone still standing ready as she climbed the steps once again and waited for her to come running back after she slid down. There seemed no end to the amount of laughter the sliding pond could evoke from her.

Soon the noise from the football field made it obvious that the second half had started. Harry continued to watch his daughter as she climbed the ladder, but he was getting more and more fidgety. Then a loud cheering, and the movement of the crowd, indicated that someone had scored. It must have been a touchdown, the cheering had that kind of sound to it. Suzie was skipping her way back to the ladder when Harry picked her up and spun her around a few times and she giggled happily. When he put her down he knelt beside her, Did you have fun, sweetheart?

Suzie nodded her head vigorously, Put me on the seesaw now, daddy.

Im afraid we havent time, honey. We have to go home soon.

We got time. Its not time to eat yet – sounding as if she actually knew dinner would not be ready for another hour or so.

Well no, not exactly, but daddy wanted to watch the football game for a few minutes before we have to go home.

O I dont like it. I dont wanna watch anymore – scrunching her face into a complete pout. We only been here a few minutes. I wanna stay here – her voice on the brink of a sob.

Ah please, sweetheart. I/ll tell you what. I/ll carry you piggy back all the way. Hows that?

We could stay here and you could carry me piggyback. You said we/d go to the playground. You said – lowering her head, still pouting, her voice even closer to tears.

Look, I know what. How about a nice surprise after dinner? How about that?

What sprize?

O, I cant tell you that. Then it wont be a surprise.

She looked up at him for a moment, still pouting, Honest? A sprize?

Of course – feeling a blush warming his face – I wouldnt lie to my little girl.

One more slide?

O.K. – standing up and following her to the ladder. When she reached the bottom he knelt and his daughter climbed on Harrys back after he cautioned her to hold on tight to his neck, but not to choke him.

He walked toward the field quickly, holding his daughters legs, then broke into a jogging lope as Suzie prodded him with a giddyup, she enjoying the breeze on her face as she put her cheek next to her daddys and relished not having to bend her head backwards to look up at people, even being able to look down at many.

Harry swiftly worked his way back to his previous spot and found out that the score was now tied. He immediately became completely involved in the game as one team put the ball in play on their own 20 after a touchback, and the fullback picked up 12 quick yards on a draw play. After that the quarterback moved his team upfield by continually outthinking the defense with trap plays and slants off the tackles and guards, and a couple of short hook passes at just the right time.

His daughter remained satisfied with the novelty of her position and her daddy moved around just enough to make it interesting. For a while. Then the novelty faded, just as the defense recovered a fumble inside their own 20 – and just when they were really moving the ball too.

I wanna go on the swings again, daddy – tapping him on the head with her hand.

I told you, Suzie, not now – what a jerk. A few more plays and they wouldve been over.

Suzie bounced up and down repeating, Please more – tugging at Harrys neck.

Not now, and stop that. Youre hurting daddy – lets see what this other quarterback can do. If he can get them out – I said stop – turning to look at Suzie. Do you want me to put you down?

No – still bouncing but no longer tugging at his neck – but I wanna go on the swings, you said – slowly pouting the words – I was hardly on them.

A time out was called and Harry knelt and his daughter slid off his back and he held her hands as he spoke softly, but firmly, to her, his irritation growing. I told you if you are a good girl I would give you a surprise after dinner. We have to go home soon – glancing at his watch – and we dont have time to go back to the playground. Now be a good girl and dont bother daddy for few minutes and I/ll piggyback you home and youll get a nice surprise after dinner. O.K.?

What sprize daddy?

Youll see after dinner – time was back in – now climb on daddys back and be a good girl. Harry stood up with Suzie on his shoulders and decided he had enough time to watch at least the next series of downs before he had to start home, and perhaps more if this guy didnt move the team. His daughter hung on quietly for a few minutes then started jiggling up and down and then jabbering and asking questions, wanting to know what they were doing and why they ran after the boy and when they were going back to the swings ... and Harry grunted a few answers while moving along the sidelines as the teams moved down the field, occasionally telling Suzie not to choke him, her whining increasing his irritation. Then Suzie started humming to herself and rocking her head back and forth as she jiggled up and down and Harry started getting angry and squeezed her leg and yelled at her to stop as she fell forward and banged her head on his and Suzie hung completely motionless for a second, stunned from the blow and Harrys voice, then started whimpering and Harry fought his anger and knelt and rubbed her head for a moment and told her not to cry. She was still whimpering slightly, asking to go back to the swings, when the quarterback threw a perfect strike to his running back and he went in for the score. Harry decided to go home as it was a little after 2.

When they were out of the crowd he wiped Suzies face with his handkerchief, We dont want mommy to know we were crying now do we?

We going home now, daddy?

Yes, honey.

Can we go on the swings first, huh?

No.

Please. I hardly didnt get to go.

No, its too late – the sadness in her voice causing Harry to respond angrily – dinners ready now. He paused and took a deep breath, thinking how his wife would react to Suzies complaint. He smiled, But dont forget I promised you a piggyback ride all the way home. O.K.?

And a sprize you said.

Yes, I wont forget. Youll get a surprise. Now climb on and we/ll go home.

Harry played horsie to his daughters giddyup and between that and an occasional tickle Suzie was laughing when they romped into the house.

Well, its about time you two vagabonds got home – taking her daughter off Harrys back, kissing her before putting her down – a few more minutes and you would have had a catastrophe instead of a roast.

Hmmmm, smells good. I guess we had better get washed. Come on honey, lets get our hands and face washed.

Ethel set the table while they washed and by the time they came back into the kitchen it was filled with savory smells, the table set, and the roast waiting for Harry to carve.

As Harry carved, Ethel put Suzie in her highchair and asked her to tell her all about the park. Were there other children there?

Uhuh. We watched a game. I was on daddys back.

A game? Didnt you go to the playground, Harry?

Of course, of course. We just stopped for a minute on the way home to watch a football game. I dont even know who was playing.

O Harry, you and football. Dont you get enough on t.v.?

It was just for a minute – here give me your plate. Heres a nice center piece.

And daddys giving me a sprize.

What is this about a surprise?

I thought we/d get some I-C-E C-R-E-A-M after dinner. You know –

Cause I was a good girl at the game, wasnt I daddy?

Thats a good girl – putting her dinner in front of her – Now you eat this all up.

Whats the sprize daddy?

Now I told you a dozen times, after dinner.

Take it easy, Harry.

Well, ever since I mentioned it shes been haunting me about it.

Well, lets forget about it and enjoy our dinner.

Ethel and Harry started eating their Sunday dinner, but Suzie just toyed with her food, I want my sprize.

Now you listen to me, young lady –

Harry. Dont lose your temper.

But Ive been hearing this all day – Suzie had lowered her head and watched and listened –

But getting yourself upset isnt going to do any good. Youll just ruin our dinner. Relax honey. I/ll take care of Suzie. Now you be a good little girl and eat your dinner. Ethel separated the food on Suzies plate into individual piles and told her to start eating.

Suzie pouted, I was a good girl.

Well, you just continue to be a good girl and eat.

I want my sprize.

You listen to mommy – glancing at Harry, noticing his face redden – and eat. If you dont eat like a good girl youll not only get no surprise, but daddy wont take you to the park again. Now you wouldnt like that, would you?

Suzie toyed with her food for a few minutes, then started whimpering very softly, a few tears slowly rolling down her cheeks. Ethel reached over with her napkin and wiped her face dry. Now you dont have to cry, honey, no one is yelling at you. I dont understand why you are so upset. We just want you to eat your dinner. Now stop crying for mommy. Ethel turned to Harry, What happened at the park, Harry, Ive never seen her in such a state? Harry glared at her, mouth jammed shut.

Suzie continued to whimper softly and shook slightly with a sob. Good girl. I want my sprize.

Harry slammed his fork down on the table and jerked himself up, Goddamn it! I/ll give you a surprise – reaching over to her plate, scooping up a handful of mashed potatoes with gravy and slapping it on her head – Heres your surprise! Ethel and Suzie just stared at Harry, their mouths open, potatoes and gravy slowly sliding down the sides of Suzies face, and then she started crying hysterically. Good! Good! Cry and get it over with! Ethel hugged Suzie as she continued to stare at the potatoes and gravy dripping from Harrys hand.

A Little Respect

Morris pushed the papers on his desk into piles, any old pile, and rushed to the elevators. He hated those last minute phone calls. He never could figure out why people waited until five to five to call. He rushed to the elevator, looking at his watch. He could still make the 5/20 if there were no more hangups. The first two elevators went right past his floor because they were filled and he groaned inwardly. He kept looking at his watch, but it didnt seem to do any good so he lit a cigarette and put it out when an elevator stopped and the doors opened. He squeezed himself in and the elevator went directly to the ground floor.

He rushed to the subway and stood on the platform constantly looking at his watch complaining loudly to himself about the service, and what in the hells keeping the train, wishing he could light a cigarette. The more he looked at his watch the more convinced he became that he would miss the 5/20 and end up on the damn 5/30, the cattle car. Eventually the train came in and he pushed and was pushed into the car. He was jammed so close to the guy in front of him that the guys mustache kept tickling Morrises nose, and whoever it was behind him must have had spaghetti and meat balls for lunch with extra garlic. He wondered what time it was.

Everybody flooded out of the train when they reached the terminal and Morris rushed, almost running, toward the proper track. He glanced at his watch and the clocks on the wall and knew it was hopeless. It was already 5/21 and it would take him at least five more minutes to get there no matter how fast he walked and god knows that if they ever left on time they would today. When he got there at 5/15, never, but today...The end of the train was just barely visible when he got to the track. He looked at the dark tunnel for a moment feeling and listening to his heart pound. He bought a paper and waited.

A cattle car, thats what the 5/30 is, a cattle car. And not only that, the 5/30 doesnt know what a schedule is ... not even a nodding acquaintance. Who knows what time I/ll get home.

When he reached his station he almost stopped for a moment to breathe the air, but decided to continue rushing to the bus stop, sneaking a few looks at his watch. The bus was there in a matter of minutes and thank god he got a seat. He read about a flood, a hatchet murder, an earthquake that killed 10,000 people, and relaxed.

The short walk to the house was almost pleasant. He looked forward to sitting and taking it easy for a few minutes, if possible, before dinner. The street was relatively quiet, quiet enough to hear the birds. Morris liked to hear the birds. It was so bucolic, like the city was a million miles away. Nice.

He opened the door of his home and was immediately ASSAULTED by the sound of machine guns, cannons and the screams of planes. His 10 year old son Milton was sitting on the floor in the living room surrounded by a few empty bowls and numerous candy wrappers. There were crumbs of crackers, popcorn and potato chips everywhere. Morris stuck his head in the doorway, Hi Miltie, how are you?

Milton stared at the screen.

Morris looked at him for a moment then raised his voice slightly, I said hello. How are you?

Milton stared at the screen.

Morris stared at his son, but couldnt outlast him. Turn it down Miltie.

Milton stared at the screen.

Miltie, I said to turn it down, its too loud. Morrises head was raging, but he just stood over his son, squeezing his newspaper, raising his voice just a little each time he spoke.

His son continued to stare at the screen.

Finally there was a commercial break and Morris tried again, Milton lower the volume.

Milton finally acknowledged his fathers presence by giving him his best Fonzie posture, without getting up. Be cool, eh?

I/ll be cool – grabbing for the control unit and Milton holding tight with both hands. Give me that you –

Look out, look out, ya jerk, ya wanna break it?

I/ll break your head you little –

Morrises wife Maya yelled from the kitchen, Is that you Morris?

He stood up, Yes. Its me.

The movie suddenly came back on with an artillery barrage that caused Morris to drop his paper. He retreated to the kitchen.

Milton stared at the screen.

Maya was turning back the aluminum foil on the t.v. dinners, Dinner will be ready in 20 minutes. A special treat. Yeah?

Your favorite, Salisbury steak. Morris nodded, With home-made water? What? Nothing. What was all that noise, were you yelling at Miltie again? Yelling? How could you tell? I heard you. How could you hear me over that racket? Maya I tell you somethings got to be done. Done? About what? About what? About Miltie. Why, what did he do now? What did he do? Thats it, he doesnt do anything. He doesnt say hello, he doesnt say goodbye. He doesnt say anything. He just sits in front of the television like a blob. He likes it, Morris. And anyway, it keeps him out of trouble. Im his father. He should say hello. Is that something terrible, to want your son, your only child, to say hello? I work all day. I work hard. Like a slave – Maya was nodding her head and continued to nod as she put the dinners back in the oven, Morris following her around the kitchen – to give my family a nice house in the suburbs so you dont have to live in the crowded city. Am I asking for a bugle call when I come home? Am I asking for trumpets and kettledrums? All Im asking for is a little consideration, thats all. Is it asking so much to have him say hello? I always say hello. You say hello, but does he? Maybe I should get a tape recorder and have him say once, only once, hello dad, and then youll play it when I come home. Maya shrugged, Excuse me, Morris, I want to set the table. Maya set the table and Morris continued to follow her around, Im going to make some changes around here. Im going to get some respect from my son. Do you hear? I hear you, Morris, and youre right. You should get some respect. Excuse me while I get the silverware. From now on, when I get home hes to turn that thing off and say hello. Maya nodded, How was your day today? My day? My day? The days I survive very well, its the nights that arent so good. The timer started ringing and Maya took the dinners from the oven. Tell Miltie its time to eat. Morris went into the living room, grim determination steeling his resolve. Come to dinner, Milton.

Bring it here.

What do you mean, bring it here?

Milton slowly turned his head and looked at his father as if he were an imbecile, then turned back to the screen.

Morris stared at his son for a moment then spun around and went back to the kitchen. He wont come to dinner. He isnt hungry? He wants to be served in there. Maya shrugged. Let him eat in there. I/ll fix a tray so ... What do you mean let him? Morris, dont get so excited, its bad for your digestion. Here, sit and relax. Maya pushed Morris into his seat and then quickly fixed a tray for Milton and took it to him. She came back and served the food and sat and smiled at Morris. Come on, Morris, eat while its hot. Morris was continually shaking his head. Bring it here, bring it here. All the cannons and machine guns in the movie seemed to be exploding in his head. Through the trauma of the cannonading he heard his sons voice and Maya got up and cut a big piece of pie and put a big scoop of ice cream on it and took it to Milton. Morris was eating. He could feel the food. He chewed. He swallowed. He must be eating. Maya sat down. He could see her, but somehow she wasnt there. Was/wasnt. Thoughts stabbed his head. They broke through his skull. Pierced his nose and ears. They spewed forth from his mouth and wrapped themselves around his head and squeezed at his throat. Some respect you can say hello Im your father I work all day the 5/30s a cattle train for what a broadside of guns and planes a little respect I dont have to listen therell be changes – Morris, you alright? – yes, some changes and then the respect without the bombs – Morris stood up, tall and straight, stiff – Maya looked up at him as she continued eating – right now we/ll start with the changes, and he strode forth from the kitchen, right past Mayas frown, and into the living room, past the blob of Milton sitting, staring, and yanked the t.v. cord from the plug and started wheeling the set out of the room.

Milton yelled. Hey, whatta ya doin?

Doing? Im making some changes.

Hey ma, MA!!!!

Maya rushed to the living room. Whats wrong? Milton was yanking at his fathers arm, hitting him, tugging at the set and yelling, NO, NO, GIVE ME THE SET!

Be careful I dont give you what you deserve. Whats going on? Morris what? – out of my way. Out! He pushed his son and Maya automatically stepped aside as Morris heaved the set out the front door and dumped it on the lawn. Maya and Milton watched as he went to the garage, From now on therell be changes, hahahahahahaha, I/ll get a hello, hahahahahaha!!!! He came out of the garage with a can of gasoline and an axe. He continued laughing hoarsely and screaming as he attacked the set with the axe, the tube exploding, huge hunks of glass scattering everywhere, Morris getting a few cuts on his hands that started bleeding, Maya and Milton screaming, Milton yanking on his mothers arm, STOPIM, STOPIM!!!! and then ran into the house, still screeching, and called the police.A few neighbors peeked out of their windows, and then came out to watch Morris chop up the t.v. set, laughing and laughing, little splotches of blood swinging from his hands, then more neighbors came out of their homes as phone calls were made to spread the news, and they came closer and closer until almost a hundred people were lined up on the sidewalk and street watching Morris as he finally stopped chopping to pour the gasoline over the shattered set and toss a match on it and the fire started with a loud POOUUFFFF, HAHAHAHAHAHAHAHAHAHAHAHA BURN YOU BAS-TARD, BURN, BURN, BURN!!!!!!!!! and he started jumping up and down and Milton ran toward the fire and Maya held him back and a couple of the neighbors children screamed, Put it out, put it out!!! and their parents started chanting, Burn, burn, burn, burn!!! and then more of the neighbors applauded and came closer to the fire, cheering Morris as he continued chanting BURN YOU BASTARD, BURN YOU BASTARD, and a siren was heard in the distance and got louder and louder and before the cops got to Morris and Maya the fire engine came screeching around the corner and two firemen came running over with extinguishers as one cop was asking Maya what was going on and Milton jumped up and down screaming KILLIM! KILLIM!!! then suddenly ran into the house and got his video camera and the other cop was trying to drag Morris away from the fire and he kept shaking the cop off yelling, Leave me alone, you have no right, burn you bastard, now he/ll say hello, and the cop dragged harder and harder and Morris resisted stronger and stronger and finally the cop turned on him, Youd better take it easy buddy or I/ll break ya head open, and then called his partner and they grabbed Morris and twisted his arms as he flailed and jumped and screamed and the three of them rolled on the lawn, the firemen telling them to look out and get out of the way as neighbors applauded Morris and booed the cops. The cops had torn almost all the clothes off Morris and finally got him face down on the lawn, Morris bruised and bleeding, and one had his nightstick pressed, hard, against the back of Morrises neck as the other one cuffed his hands behind his back and Milton was busy filming the scene on his tape machine and Maya stood quietly watching as the cops dragged Morris, still laughing/screaming, to the patrol car and the firemen spread the ashes and made certain the fire was out before leaving.

Milton spent the night with his grandparents. He hooked his tape machine to their set and watched the cops drag his father away, laughing hysterically and shaking his fist at the screen, Killim, Killim, Killim!!! then played the tape over and over and over . . .

Puberty

The boy leaned against the fender of a car bouncing a rubber ball lightly on the palm of his hand . . . then bounced it on the ground hitting the crack between his feet, four, five, six, seven times, unaware of his actions, his eyes staring, his movements automatic.

He stopped bouncing the ball and just held it, his hands hanging at his side, unconsciously squeezing the ball. He had always had a special feeling about a ball, not just that it meant he would soon be with his friends and a game would start, but something more personal. He not only loved the feel and texture, he loved the smell and the sound it made as it hit the pavement or a wall, or was being hit by a bat or a hand, each sound different and special. Sometimes, if he had a ball long enough, he would wash it, and though it never looked the same as a new one, it had its own particular look and he loved it. And though he never defined the feeling all these things about a ball evoked in him, he experienced it whenever he tapped it lightly in the air or bounced it on the ground as he walked. And now that joy was not only absent, he didnt even know that it was missing, aware only of a hollowness within him.

On Saturday he always rushed through breakfast and ran to the schoolyard (time measured as the distance between Saturdays, each long hour of school that passed bringing Saturday nearer), and now he stood on Third Avenue staring at the ball. He had always been the first in the schoolyard yet the others had been there for hours and he still stood on the avenue, only a block away, wondering why he didnt want to join them and why he felt so strange. . . so sad.

He threw his ball against a building, caught it, then put it in his pocket and slowly started walking. The avenue was crowded with the usual weekend shoppers rushing from store to store, testing fruits and vegetables, asking questions, stopping to talk with each other, young children wiggling in strollers and tugging at arms . . . and the trolleys, trucks and cars made the same accustomed noises. Even the little old Italian man with the pushcart of snails was there today with a group of kids standing around watching and laughing as the snails crawled on the sides of the pushcart, the little vendor picking them up and dropping them back into the baskets. The boy ignored a call from one of the kids and continued walking through the crowd, puzzled by the strange feeling that seemed to be responsible for his being on the avenue instead of the schoolyard, and not watching, as he had always joyfully done, the snails and the way the vendor plucked them off the sides of the cart and twirled his gigantic mustache after dropping them in the baskets. For the first time in all the years he had been fascinated by the man and his pushcart he didnt wonder if his mustache smelled of snails. It seemed wrong, for some inexplicable reason, for him to be here (had he always thought about his mustache?) instead of the schoolyard, yet he could find no new desires to replace the ones that had formed the boundaries, as well as the center, of his world.

He left the avenue and walked down 69th Street, stopping in front of the firehouse and joining the onlookers watching the firemen clean the trucks and test the equipment. Hoses were stretched up and down the street, men were shining and polishing brass, a spotlight was turned on and spun in an arc, the huge ladder raised and directed against the side of the building, men climbing up . . .

The boy watched, without excitement, and started to take the ball from his pocket . . . then shoved it back and walked away, not turning as he heard the grinding of gears and the whish of water, continuing down the street, looking at the familiar houses and stores, feeling more and more the uneasy urgency in his body and strange weighted feeling in his chest.

He looked around and nothing was different and that puzzled him. Something within him demanded that the street, the buildings, the people be different, yet they were all the same but now he lacked identity with them. The footprints he had left on these streets all the thousands of times he had walked them were gone, they no longer felt like his streets, yet he continued to wander through them seemingly seeking something without the slightest idea what it might be, not knowing for sure if he was looking for something or really trying to get away. He felt the need for companionship yet was driven to aloneness, unable to ask why, nor sure that there was a question to ask, wandering through the suffocating point in time where the old is left behind before the new is even known to exist; that point where even memories cannot be evoked, only vaguely felt without comfort.

He stopped and watched a cat rummaging through a garbage can, its scars and matted fur symbols of its valiant fight against all who would try to kill it, and of its devotion to its kittens (feeling that the cat did not want simply to satisfy its hunger, but was looking for food to feed its young hidden from harm in a dark cellar) and he wanted to pick it up and pet it, take it home, wash it, feed it, listen to it purr as it lapped milk . . . take it to bed with him and feel its soft fur as it snuggled close to him . . .

he could even put a little bell around its neck and watch it chase a ball or rubber mouse and listen to the tinkle . . .

and no one would hurt Lucky. He wouldnt be chased by kids throwing rocks. They wouldnt spin him by the tail and toss him high in the air. Lucky wouldnt have to claw his way free from rough hands and run panicky down the street dodging between legs and parked cars . . . being crushed by the wheels of a truck. He had to help her! He walked toward the cat but it instinctively jerked its head up, looked for a second, then sprang from the can and ran. He didnt try to chase it but watched it run down the street, sad that the cat had not understood.

The cat disappeared and the boy stood staring for a moment, then slowly continued down the street, watching his shadow dim the cracks in the pavement, the bottle caps, scraps of paper, popsicle sticks and old pieces of chewing gum that had been ground into the cement. He turned the corner and walked along Colonial Road to Bliss Park. He met another kid at the entrance who walked beside him. See Rusty taday?

The boy shook his head.

Ya think hes here?

Dont know, Joey.

I got a couple a broken light bulbs in here – rattling a paper bag and grinning – I hope hes aroun.

The boy nodded and they continued walking down the path, across the grass and stopped under a large berry tree and ate some berries, the boy feeling the warm, sweet juice trickle down his throat and enjoying the flavor which somehow made him feel even sadder. The other boy grabbed handfuls and chomped them happily, aint they great? Man, I could eat a million ofem.

They continued walking across the grass, the boy enjoying the feel of it under his feet; looking at the sky and trees; hearing the voices of kids, their mothers; of skaters on the paths; the sudden yells of ball players; the sound of his steps on the grass; the rustle of branches and leaves; the sight and the sound of the birds . . .

His loneliness didnt decrease, but he felt more content within his feeling of isolation, as if such a feeling belonged here with the grass and trees.

Hey, look, there he is. Joey was pointing to a group of a few men and a couple of boys sitting on the side of the hill. When they reached the group they sat with the other kids who were laughing and yelling at Rusty to feed the squirrels. Rusty waved his hand at them and took a drink of wine from a bottle, still in the brown paper bag, then passed it to the guy next to him. There were three of them and they continued to pass the bottle.

Joey shook his bag in front of the other kids then said to Rusty, I brought ya somethin ta eat. They all laughed and he shook the bag again before giving it to Rusty. Rusty opened it and looked at the pieces of broken light bulbs, took another drink, passed the bottle and wiped his mouth with the back of his hand, Jesus Christ, could ya spare it? He ripped open the bag and laid it on the ground. Ya know, when I was with the circus they used ta serve it on a tray. He burst out laughing and the kids laughed and the boy could feel his face starting to smile but something within him fought against it. Rusty stopped laughing and picked up a large piece of glass and put it in his mouth and started chewing. The kids stared, their eyes getting wider and wider. He swallowed and licked his lips, Musta been a GE. Can always tell a GE. They got a Michigan taste. He burst into another laugh, stopping when the bottle was passed back to him. He ate all the glass in the bag, the kids watching him, amazed no matter how many times they had seen him do the same thing. The boy watched too, transfixed, aware of what he was watching yet that little something that turned the viewing into amazement was missing and he didnt even wonder what happened to all that glass in Rustys stomach.

When Rusty had finished the glass he folded the bag and gently wiped his lips with it and said, My compliments to the chef. The kids giggled and laughed.

One of the kids handed him a few peanuts, Feed the squirrels, Rusty. Rusty took the peanuts and giggled, then crawled a few feet away and held out a peanut to a squirrel who had just descended a tree. The squirrel looked for a moment, then took a few steps toward Rusty who threw the nut to him. The squirrel picked it up, examined it carefully, then scooted off and buried it. Rusty crawled after him and when the squirrel left Rusty dug up the nut and held it up in the air – the kids screeching and laughing – then put it in his mouth and crawled back to the group, everyone laughing loudly, the boy smiling, the other kids yelling and slapping each other. Rusty sat up, the nut in his mouth, his arms extended, hands dangling, and cheeped, then turned and crawled away looking for another squirrel. The boy watched feeling his face fighting to giggle, to laugh. His hands wanted to clap and slap one of the other kids on the back, but the oppressive weight on his chest made it all impossible, and the unfamiliar feeling within let him know that there is no joy, no reason to laugh and so he felt even more cut off from his friends and his familiar world.

He left the group and walked slowly up the hill, hearing the screeching of bluejays mingling with the voices and laughter, to the open summer house on top, standing for a moment in its shade watching a squirrel running spirally up a tree, then walking to the stone wall around the seaside perimeter of the hill. He sat on the wall and looked at the harbor . . . watching the tugs towing barges of mud, coal, railroad cars, white smoke coming from the tall stacks and small black rings pumping from the short stubby ones . . . the ferries entering and leaving their slips . . . the cars moving along the parkway . . . the people walking along Shore Road . . . the kids running, their kites slowly staggering up as they yanked the string . . .

then dropped from the wall and walked down the hill to the shore.

He walked along the shore looking across the bay at the Staten Island shoreline. He watched and listened to the waves slapping lightly against the seawall and whirling between the rocks, leaving bits of wood and debris amongst them when it ebbed, the next swell picking them up again and bobbing them on its peak before breaking on the rocks and slapping the seawall, then folding back on itself and whirling between the rocks as it returned to its source, once again leaving behind the unwanted debris.

He stopped, leaned on the railing running along the edge of the seawall and stared at the water . . . hearing the clang of the ferry mooring winch, the bell buoys, the horns and whistles of the ships in the bay . . . thinking of the sadness, loneliness, (but none of the adventure) that has always been associated with the sea . . . feeling a connection between himself and that loneliness . . .

He looked down at the rocks and the small crabs crawling over and between them, remembering the previous summer when he and his friends sat here for hours catching them, throwing most of them back, saving a few to scare the girls with . . . . But it all seemed unreal now . . . not as if it had never happened, but as if it had happened in some remote age or different life, there seeming to be no connection between then and now. Nor did he find any joy in the vague memory, feeling only more saddened and depressed.

He lifted his head and looked at the Narrows ... then gazed toward the sea. The horizon seemed strangely significant, but trying to define it only confused his thoughts more ....

Once (it couldnt have been too long ago) he and his friends came here on a gray day when the water was dark and whipped with whitecaps, the waves crashing against the rocks and seawall, the spray leaping above the railing and cascading down on them as they held fast to the railing, moving instinctively with the swaying of the ship, the boy yelling orders to his crew as the ship lurched dangerously close to the rocks in the violent and uncharted sea. He refused to turn his back to the biting spray but remained steadfast at his post, ignoring the water as it lashed his face, barking the crucial orders that would bring the ship safely through the storm ...

Many times he thought happily of that day and whenever the wind blew and the water in the bay kicked up and the spray lashed the wall, he would try to get his friends to go with him to the shore, but something always prevented it and so he never relived it except in his mind, remembering each wave and tasting once again the salt as he felt the spray sting his face.

He tried reliving it now, and though each time in the past the old joy and excitement not only returned but increased, he now remembered only that it had happened and nothing more. That day was dead.

He turned from the bay feeling deserted (for if he could find no joy here or even raise its memory, where could it be found?) and walked back to Third Avenue. The plaintiveness and tragedy of before were completely inside him now and he felt the sadness of the world within him, feeling every tear that had ever rolled down a cheek flooding his being, and though a part of him tried to fight this sadness the effort was weak. It seemed right for the worlds misery to flow through him because he was, in some unknown way, responsible for its pain.

He stood on the corner for a moment wondering what there was he could do ...

where he could go ...

feeling completely isolated from the people walking by yet sensing a new relationship between himself and them.

He turned and instinctively walked toward home, feeling strangely conspicuous among the people, as if he were wearing a mask that advertised his feelings. He looked at the people, expecting them to stop talking and smiling and laughing and stand there, just stand there and stare at him.

He lowered his eyes and walked a little faster (vaguely wondering why they were laughing – could he laugh?). Surely Mom can help. He could always run to her and put his arms around her, tell her what was wrong, what was troubling him. She would comfort him, reassure him. Maybe that was all that was needed, just to cry and have Mom kiss him, hug him, and everything would be alright, nothing changed, nothing to fear????

The boy stopped and looked across the avenue at the entrance of the apartment house, his eyes tearing .... He did not hear the noises of the cars, the trucks, the trolleys, the people, but an etherized drone ...

the newsstand next to the doorway whirled and the traffic on the avenue blurred into a meaningless mass ....

Why couldnt he run across the street and up the stairs to Mom? Why couldnt he move????

Tears fell from his eyes, his lungs and chest felt like they were collapsing.

Was he sitting?

Standing?

lying anesthetized, strapped to a table and slowly losing

consciousness with a mask clamped tightly on his face listening
to a repetitious drone of final words

                              loud then soft

                                            loud then
soft, dragging, spinning, dragging . . .

                                                      The
drone whirled to a highspeed whine

                              poles reversing

                                            orbits tilting
flashing suns and planets spinning away

                                            colliding,
bursting

          showering spermlike sparks . . . .

                              A groan of
overwhelming agony screamed through him and rattled in his
throat. His head jerked up and he turned and staggered to the
corner . . .

          then fled in panic down the street past the people
standing and talking, past the walkers and the women with their
baby carriages, past the trees and the parked cars, and past the
yells of ball players in the schoolyard . . .

The Coat

Harry loved his coat. He had gotten it toward the end of winter and it saved his life. The winters on the Bowery were tough under any conditions, but without a coat the winters were deadly, bodies picked up each morning, some frozen to the ground and having to be chipped loose. But Harrys coat became more than comfort, more than protection against the cold, even more than a life saver . . . it was his friend, his buddy . . . his only companion. He dearly loved his coat.

It was long, reaching almost to his ankles, and heavy, and he could wrap it around himself almost twice and when he raised the collar he felt completely protected from the world. It was an Army surplus coat that he had gotten from the Salvation Army, one of the last ones they had. He loved it right away. But keeping a coat on skid row during the winter was not easy. He had to be alert. There was always some person, or group, ready to take it from you and they were willing to kill you for it.

But now the weather was getting warmer and he could relax a little. He didnt get careless, but it would be progressively easier to protect his coat. He had seen men sell their coats when the weather warmed, for enough for a bottle of wine, but he would never be that foolish. Winter always returned. He had spent part of one winter with newspapers wrapped around his body trying desperately to keep out the cold, each day an eternity, but that was only a memory he kept alive during the heat of summer when keeping the coat seemed such a burden. Winter always returned.

During the cold weather he often worked as a dishwasher at

night. When he first got to the row a couple of old-timers tried to show him how to panhandle, how to size up a mark and know whether to lookim in the eye and tellim you need a drink, or try the painful look and old vet approach, and all the variations. And they warned him that the most important thing was to know who not to hit. They have a look in their eye and theyre liable to killya. You gotta stay clear ofem ... And Harry would watch them panhandle, always staying south of Houston Street – the cops dont botherya down here, but north of Houstons bad news – but Harry just could not go up to a stranger and ask him for money. He even had a difficult time, finding it almost impossible, to ask for his money after a nights work. He had been that way all his life and had given up trying to change.

He liked to work at night because it not only gave him a job, but a place to stay warm during the long, cold nights. It was easier to find a place that was safe during the day to drink his wine and sleep. When he worked he always hung his coat next to the sink and watched it the whole evening. No one was supposed to be back there, except him, but that was no guarantee that someone wouldnt suddenly rush in and try to grab his coat.

Being alone was another reason he liked washing dishes. It was just him and the dishes, and his coat. Harry always had a difficult time being with people, having left school early because of the daily terror of being with so many people in one room and having to stand and talk when called on. He just spent more time by himself and less and less in school and eventually they left him alone and he drifted away, spending as much time as possible alone, longing always for companionship, never able to talk about his fear, no one, including Harry, understanding why he did what he did.

The nights washing dishes went easy enough. He had his warmth, some food, his solitude, and he would take a drink from time to time, being sure no none saw him take the bottle from his pocket. Survival depended upon keeping certain things secret. And dishwashing jobs were always available. Its not the kind of job guys keep. Some place always needed a dishwasher.

When he finished work he would get breakfast and his money,

then buy a bottle of muscatel and find an abandoned building somewhere safe. The rest of the row was waking up and starting their day and he could nestle somewhere and not worry about people stumbling on him. He always went as far back in the deserted buildings as possible. There were gangs that roamed the Bowery who were worse than crazed dogs and you had to be careful you didnt let anyone think you had something they might want. He always put his bottle in the huge pocket of his coat and walked as aimlessly as possible. He didnt know how many men he had seen beaten, and killed, for a coat or a bottle of wine.

You had to be careful on skid row. You had to be your own council . . . your own friend.

He climbed over the rubble and garbage in an empty lot to an abandoned building and worked his way around battered walls and fallen beams to a distant corner in the shadows and sat, wrapped his coat around him, and opened his bottle. He took a long drink, almost half the bottle, then gulped air for a moment, then let out a long sigh . . . He looked at the bottle admiringly . . . affectionately, as he felt the wine warming his gut and flowing through his system . . . then took another quick drink . . . then another . . . then licked his lips as he put the top on the bottle and placed it carefully beside him. He took out his money and rolled it up, except for a dollar, and shoved it through a small hole in a pocket into the lining where it could not be found, then leaned back against the wall, wrapped his coat around him, cradled the bottle on his lap, holding it tightly, closed his eyes and smiled and wiggled as he felt the wine going through his body, feeling nice and warm and sending a glow through him right down to the tips of his toes.

Fantasies used to come with the wine, but somewhere, sometime, they stopped, or maybe they just drifted away. There just did not seem to be any energy available to bring them back and no material for new ones. All hopes, fantasies, dreams, now centered on this one moment of Harry and his bottle nestling safely and warmly in the corner of an abandoned building . . .

But there were memories that sometimes haunted him . . . or others that eased their way across his minds eye with gentle waves of pleasure ...

He was driving through the Appalachians once when he pulled off road to watch a sunset. He watched the sun go out of sight, then the changing layers of colors turned from pink to red, from blue to purple, sitting alone, tears rolling from his eyes and down his cheeks as he was overwhelmed by the beauty of the incredible spectacle ... sitting there still when there was only a faint hint of blue/gray in the distance as it got darker, and when the moons brightness started to bring light to the valley below and the sky softened into a thick dark velvet, twinkling stars slowly emerged and dotted the darkened sky, he was still there immersed and transfixed by the wonder of it, experiencing its beauty and miracle in some secret place deep within him ...

But much time had passed since he was last visited by that memory.

He took another drink, recapped the bottle and looked around ... He had everything he needed right now. A bottle ... a place to park himself for a while ... and his coat ... his wonderful, beautiful coat. He kissed the collar, I love you coat, and chuckled. He took another drink and closed his eyes and felt the warmth, then looked at his coat. I can always depend on you. Youre my friend. My really true friend. My buddy. You/ll never let me down, right? And I/ll never let you down. I swear to you – raising his right hand in a solemn oath – I/ll never let you down. Unto the death I/ll never let you down. He lowered his hand and took another drink, then looked at something shining in the darkness. He stared hard, frowning, until he finally made out the form of a huge rat staring at him. A shock of disgust and fear sickened him and he closed his eyes and huddled deeper into his coat, then opened his eyes, but the rat was still there, his eyes looking like two beacons in the dark. He stared at the eyes, swallowing a mounting nausea, then forced himself to pick up a piece of debris and throw it at the rat, the rat quickly disappearing in the dark. He took another drink and relaxed. At least it was real. If it wasnt he couldnt have gotten rid of it so easily. He had had d.t./s, but he never saw anything like rats. He knew some guys did and he didnt know how they survived imagining that rats were crawling all over them . . . he shook his head, Arghhh. He opened his bottle and threw the top away, took a long drink, then pulled his coat even tighter around him. He cant bother us, can he? He/d never be able to get me. My buddy would keep him away, wouldntya? Nothin, no one . . . no one, nothin. Right? Cant bother us. He snuggled deeper into the corner and his coat. He closed his eyes momentarily and listened to the wine singing through his body and smiled, then started singing, Nights are long since – he started giggling and nodding his head – I dream about you all thru – he started laughing – hehehehehe – thru –hehehehehe – ishh . . . ishh . . . my Buddy . . . my Buddy – he started waving his hand in a small arc conducting himself – Watch the bounding ball – all through the – hehehehehe . . . ishh . . . Nobody – hahaha – Nobod – ishhh – Bod – hahaha . . . he gulped and swallowed hard and shook his head – Nobody hehe – ishh . . . he took another drink, his off-key singing continuing in his head, a few mumbling words coming from his mouth, nobody but a buddy, hehehehe . . . continuing to stammer and giggle and nod his head, then emptied the bottle and tossed it as far away as possible, deep into the shadows of the rubble and listened to the tinkle of broken glass reverberate through his snug nest like the tinkling of sleigh bells as his head slowly lowered, his chin eventually resting on the lapel of his great coat, and drifting into sleep.

He moved, jerked spastically and mumbled as he was slowly dragged back to consciousness. It was much darker in the building but he was long accustomed to waking up about this same time so he knew it must be late afternoon. He got to his feet and brushed off his coat then slowly, and carefully, made his way past and through the shattered walls out of the building.

The shadows were long as he picked his way through the rubble of the lot, slipping and stumbling, rats squealing and skittering off as he staggered and inched his way to the street.

The traffic was heavy this time of the evening and Harry huddled in his coat as he walked along the street, the people fulfilling his need for human companionship without being a threat. He had spent many, many years alone, and lonely, but they had not eliminated his need, and occasional desire, to be with people. As long as he was free to just be there on the street without having to be a part of them, he was alright.

Soon he became aware of the need for a drink and he bought a bottle of muscatel, putting the bottle in his pocket before leaving the store. He rushed from the vicinity of the store and went to a deserted, safe area to take a drink. He rejoined the activity of the street, huddled deep in his coat against the cold, a feeling of triumph and love flowing through his body as he turned his back to the cold wind, aware of his bodys warmth.

He decided he would work again tonight so he made the rounds of the joints and soon was standing in front of a couple of sinks. He took his coat off and hung it right by the sink where he could keep an eye on it.

Spring passed easily enough. During the day if it got too hot in the sun he would go to the shady side of the street and though it was warm he was still able to wear his coat. A few times he was tempted to take off his coat and carry it, but he knew better. That was inviting trouble. It would be too easy for some guy to knock into him while his partner yanked the coat away from him and run down the street. No, he could not afford to take chances. No matter how hot it got, his coat was always valuable to winos. It could always be hocked for at least a jug.

And anyway, there was always the relief of the evening, his coat being perfect for the springtime coolness. Then, as the spring rains passed, everything seemed to be a little easier. For a month or so he had a great apartment. He had found a huge packing crate and spent hours dragging and pushing it to the remains of an old building. It took a tremendous amount of will to not just leave it in the first room of the building, but to push and tug it around corners and back into the recesses of the building where it would not so easily be stumbled upon. He set it up in a corner and cleared some of the debris away from it, not too large an area, he did not want it obvious that someone was living there, he did not want to leave a trail, just enough so he could roll in and out of bed without stumbling over something. And he found an old calendar, maybe 5 or 6 years old, and hung it on a wall of the crate. He collected a few rags and the remains of a cushion and made himself the semblance of a chair.

He spent as much time as possible in his apartment, loving the feeling of security and the smell of the wood, and if it was exceptionally warm, as it usually was in the summer, even at night, he would take off his coat and wrap it carefully in some old plastic sheets he had found and bury it under the rubble where it could not be seen, secure in the knowledge that no matter what happened his coat would be safe. Then he would lean back in his chair and drink and sing or talk softly to himself, or sometimes be silent and watch the various creatures that shared the abandoned buildings and lots with him, coming from deep under the buildings, from caverns of deserted cellars or basements, or perhaps deeper, from some unknown area beyond that created by man and his buildings, where darkness and moisture fostered and nurtured its strange inhabitants. He watched with fear and disgust trying, from time to time, to close his eyes and thus, eliminate them from his world, but he was more afraid of not knowing where they were, so he was forced, beyond will and desire, to watch them when they suddenly appeared, scuttled about, then froze still and looked, eyes reflecting light, eyes that seemed to get brighter and larger the longer he stared, so large and bright they appeared to leave the creatures head and float toward him ... his body tense, becoming stiff, a panic and nausea knotting and constricting his gut and throat ...

until the creatures suddenly ran, jumped, or just disappeared into the unknown and fearsome world they had come from.

Sometimes he watched, fascinated, as they would slink through the shadows and rubble, unaware of his presence, intent upon not being seen by their prey or predators. One day, while there was still faint light finding its way into the inner recesses, he watched a huge tomcat slowly, stealthily, stealing up on something. He was battered, with a piece missing from an ear and large clots of fur torn from his body. He was obviously a fighter and survivor . . . no, more than that, he was a prevailer and Harry developed an instant affection for the cat. He watched him, not knowing what it was the cat saw, but it was obviously tracking something as he crawled along the ground, his belly rubbing the stones and rubble, moving a few feet . . . stopping . . . staring . . . nose twitching, tail beating. Harry followed the direction the cat seemed to be looking, fascinated and curious, and thought he saw some sort of movement . . . then was certain there was something back in the shadows. The cat continued crawling . . . then stopped, its tail beating rapidly, his entire rear portion wiggling . . . then he leaped and Harry saw the prey as it squealed and tried to escape. It was a huge rat and it continued to squeal as the cat hit it in mid air. The rat rolled over and got to its feet quickly and found itself cornered against an old sink. The cat slowly . . . cunningly . . . forced the rat back into the corner until it could no longer move and when it leaped the cat leaped too and grabbed it with his large paws and they both landed, hard, on a piece of steel, the rat squealing so loud it almost hurt Harrys ears. The rat managed to get out of the grasp of the cat but had nowhere to go and the cat continued inching closer and closer to the now bleeding rat. Harry continued to remain immobile and stare, barely breathing, trying to shut out the sight of the blood, yet glad the rat was bleeding and had to fight himself not to shout encouragement to the cat. The rat leaped again, and the cat caught him, and this time as they landed the cat sunk his teeth into the back of the neck of the rat and shook it violently, the squealing of the rat piercing the stillness, and shook the rat until there was a loud snap and the rat was instantly silent as it hung from the jaws of the cat. He shook it a few more times, then dropped it and looked at it for a moment . . . then pushed it with a paw . . . looked for another second or two . . . pushed it around for a few minutes as if it were a ball of yarn . . . Harry becoming very uncomfortable . . . then picked it up and carried it into the shadows, out of sight, but not out of hearing, the silence broken, from time to time, with the crunching of bones. Harry clamped his hands over his ears and pinched his eyes shut . . . .

Eventually he allowed his face to relax and his eyes to slowly open . . . everything looked as before. Then he removed his hands from his ears . . . and sighed with relief at the silence. He took a long, long drink and sighed again and soon realized that his mind was back into an old habit of wondering about the violence of nature but pushed it from his mind with another long drink.

The coat was hot in the summer, even in the shade, if you could find any, but he did not mind. He knew that another winter would be here before you knew it and he was going to survive that winter. His coat would guarantee that.

He gave up his dishwashing in the summer and did a lot of junking. He got a push cart as early in the morning as possible and stayed away from the row and the gangs who might rip him off when he collected a load of paper, or after he got his money. And, when he was safely distant, he took off his coat and put it in the cart and covered it with paper.

He concentrated on paper and cardbord. He had seen some other junkmen bring in sinks and pieces of furniture and haggle with the guy and eventually get a few dollars, but when he tried it the guy told him what he had wasnt worth anything and he just nodded and went out again for a load of paper. He knew the guy was going to keep it and sell it, but he just didnt know how to bargain with him the way the other guys did. So he stayed with cardboard and paper.

He took it nice and easy, knowing he would get enough for what he needed. He always had a bottle of muscatel with him and would take a drink from time to time and go leisurely about his work. Usually he would stop in some greasy spoon and fill himself with beans and bread before going back to his apartment with a bottle of muscatel.

Eventually he had to give up his apartment. One night he came back with a bottle and before he turned the last corner he could hear voices. He stopped. Listened ... Sounded like a couple of guys, maybe more ... could be three ... but who knows? Their voices were muffled and indistinct and he could just barely make out what was happening. They were fighting over who was to get the next drink, or who got more than the other. He listened ... not moving ... the voices got louder and angrier and suddenly there was a thud and a gurgling scream, then another thud ... and another ... and he recognized the sound as someone being hit on the head with a rock or a pipe, or something similar. Then the thudding stopped and there was the sound of a falling body, and then silence ... then the sound of someone drinking ... Fear and disgust almost panicked him, but he forced himself to quietly leave. He stood in the evening air for a few moments, swallowing his nausea, wanting to get away from there as rapidly as possible, but feeling weak and sick. He took many deep breaths and closed his eyes from time to time, trying to push away the sound and the image. Soon he was able to take a drink, then work his way through the rubble to another building and find a corner to nest in and dissolve the incident in wine.

Even with the heat summer was easy time. He slowly pushed his junk cart through the streets looking around, taking an occasional drink, watching kids run and play a thousand and one games, looking at the trees, bushes, shrubs, and flowers, feeling free and unencumbered with the sun and air on his face. In the evening he would go to whatever abandoned building he was using, and drink, sing and talk softly to himself until he lost consciousness.

Then autumn turned the leaves and the breeze and he would pick up an occasional red leaf streaked with yellow. Now, with the cooler evenings his coat was always around him, keeping out the chill and keeping in the warmth, the tip of his nose cold, making him more aware of the friendliness and comfort of his companion ... his soft singing and talking not so much to himself, but more to his buddy ... his great coat.

Then the leaves stopped turning colors and fell, the trees becoming bare and naked and exposed. He sought out the sunny side of the street, constantly awake to the chill in the air that meant another winter would soon be blowing its way through the Bowery. It brought him even closer to his coat, knowing that it would protect him from that wind and the cold that would soon make the entire row shiver and nightly leave in its wake the bodies of winos who had passed out in doorways and abandoned buildings, their bodies blue and rigid.

But winter was yet to come and Harry picked his way through the rubble of a lot, happily aware of the sudden change in temperature as he walked from a sunny spot into a long shadow and then once more into the late sun. He heard voices and laughter and looked at a couple of older kids dancing around a wino staggering through the lot a short distance ahead of Harry. He saw one of the kids pouring something on the wino. Harry assumed it was water and shivered momentarily as he realized what it must feel like to the guy who was wet, but then one of the kids lit a match and tossed it at the bum and he suddenly exploded and was engulfed in flames and the kids ran away, laughing, as the wino screamed and tried to run but kept falling down. Harry reacted instantly and ran toward the bum, slipped out of his coat, quickly knocked the wino to the ground and wrapped the coat around him smothering the flames, the wino screaming in agony, Harry having to fight to keep his coat wrapped around him, but mercifully the guy soon passed out and Harry was able to suffocate the flames. He kept his coat wrapped around him to be certain the flames stayed out and to cushion his body against the sharp edges of the rubble.

Others had seen what happened and soon the police and an ambulance were there. The attendants carefully rolled the wino out of Harrys coat. He was charred, but alive. They placed him in the ambulance and then asked Harry if he was alright. Any burns? Harry shook his head. Why dont you take a ride with us and we/ll check you out at the hospital. Harry shook his head, holding his coat close to him and staring at the ambulance. The attendant shrugged, You saved his life . . . for now anyway. Dont know if it/ll do much good though.

The ambulance left and the police questioned Harry briefly. Harry clutched his coat to him, still in a state of shock. A couple of people told the police that they could describe the kids who did it, Probably the same kids whove been doin it to all the others.

Yeah, they think its some kind of game.

They call it burn a bum.

Harry managed to work himself into the coat and stumble away from the small knot of people to the liquor store. It was when he shoved the bottle in his pocket that he noticed how much his hands had been burned. The sudden pain snapped him out of his shock and he became more alert as he went to his corner nest in the abandoned building. He looked at his coat and though it had a few black spots there was no real damage done. He hugged it to his breast as his body unfolded in the corner and almost cried with relief as he leaned against the wall. He continued to hug and kiss his coat, overwhelmed by the fact that it was alright, realizing that the flames could have destroyed his coat when he wrapped it around the wino. His relief was so great that he spent many, many minutes hugging and kissing his coat, telling it he was sorry if it got hurt but he had to do it, he couldnt just let the guy burn, and his coat reassured him that it was alright, it understood and agreed that Harry had done the right thing . . .

Eventually the shock was completely drained from him and Harry put his coat on and wrapped it snuggly around him, but even the fact that his coat was safe could not stop the feeling of sadness that flowed through him. Harry took a drink and once more looked at his burned hands. They werent too bad. A little red with a couple of blisters. They were starting to hurt now. He took another long drink. Soon the wine would take away the pain. In the meantime he would hold a few cold stones in his hands to keep them cool . . .

but the cold stones, and even the wine, couldnt seem to stop that terrible sadness that was taking control of his body and mind. He took another long drink trying to drown out the screams of the winos agony, but when they finally faded he could still hear the peoples voices, its some kindda game . . . its some kindda game, its some kindda game . . . .

He suddenly groaned and tears burst forth from his eyes and he folded his arms around his head as he sobbed from the depth of his being, O God . . . O God . . . he squeezed his arms tighter around his head hoping the pressure might in some miraculous way ease the sickness flowing through his body and the pain of his mind and soul . . . O God . . . why is life so fragile???? Why???? Why????

There was still a faint glow in the sky as he walked along the street, his hands deep in his pockets, talking softly to his coat, telling it how much he loved it and appreciated how warm it was keeping him and how he never had to be afraid of the winters because of it; and sometimes he would whistle for a few minutes, or even hum, and then continue talking to his coat and tell it how theyd get a bottle of muscatel and go back to that nice warm place they had fixed up last night and just drink and sleep, no worries no cares, ju – A couple of bums suddenly shoved him in a doorway and he knew they were after his coat. He swung out and screamed HELP!!!! HELP!!!! AAAAAAAAAAAHHHHH-HHHHHHHH!!!! – Shut up ya son of a bitch – Harry continued flailing his arms, screaming, AAAAAAAAAAAAAHHHHHH-HHHHHHHH!!!! – Fa krists sake grabim – What the fuck ya think Im tryin to do – Hitim fa krists sake – and Harry continued to swing his arms and fight to get out the door, still screaming, hoping someone would come to help him, AAAAAAAAAAA-HHHHHHHHHHHHH!!!! – and the three of them continued to fall over each other and bounce off the walls in the cramped hallway, Harry flailing and screaming as he lunged for the door, the bums trying to grab him and hit him with a piece of pipe one of them was holding, and Harry finally crashed through the thin door – AAAAAAAAAAAAAHHHHHHHHHHHHHHHHH – just as the guy hit him on the head with the pipe and Harry staggered forward onto the street and the guy hit him again and Harry fell to his knees, his arms wrapped around himself so they couldnt get the coat off, and he was hit again and knocked flat on his face and was kicked, but still he kept his arms wrapped around himself in his semi-conscious state, muttering, no, no, no, as they tried to yank the coat off, and people passing by glanced at first and then looked and soon a few asked what the hell was going on and the guys looked around at the people, still tugging on the coat, and then a prowl car turned the corner and they let go of the coat and ran . . .

The cops got out of the car and walked over to where Harry was lying on the sidewalk, blood seeping from his head, his arms wrapped around his body protecting his coat in a death grip. The cops looked down at him for a moment . . . Seems to be alive.

Yeah . . . Guess we/d better put in a call.

The other cop nodded and strolled back to the car and called an ambulance.

A dozen or so people milled around Harry, asking what had happened, shaking their heads or relating what they had seen or surmised; some passersby stopped to join them or to look for a moment then move on, others slowing slightly and seeing it was just a bum hurried on their way.

The doctors did what they could for him but Harry was not expected to live through the night, and at 4 a.m. his heart actually stopped beating, but an alert nurse pounded his chest, his heart responding with a feeble but constant beat. Every function of his body was monitored and checked with amazement, there being no known medical explanation for his still being alive.

The fourth day they started having hope that he would live. Not because there had been any improvement in his condition, everything was still the same, but simply because it somehow seemed inevitable. Then, about 4/30 a.m., his body started to convulse from alcoholic withdrawal. His condition got worse and worse rapidly, yet still he lived, something inside him refusing to give up.

Treating the convulsions was in itself a simple matter but the treatment tended to aggravate his other condition, and so the hospital personnel had to maintain a delicate balance so they would not bring about his death from one condition while treating the other.

Miraculously he survived the convulsions and the treatment, and after being in a coma for a week he regained consciousness for a brief period, his eyes barely focusing, but able to nod his head when asked if he could hear, then mumbled something about his coat before drifting once again into unconsciousness. From that moment on his recovery was slow, sometimes barely discernible, but steady.

A week later he was able to talk and was visited by a clerk from the records office. She smiled and sat down next to the bed and explained that as he was unconscious, and had no identification when he was brought in, she had to ask him a few questions. Alright? Do you feel up to it?

He nodded. They didnt get my coat, did they?

What? What coat?

The one I was wearing. They tried to get my coat.

Oh . . . . Im sure its down in the clothing room just like all the others.

The information seemed to take a while to register, but eventually it did and he sighed inwardly . . . then nodded his head.

Now then, I need a little information. It wont take long. Name?

Harry. Harry Wright.

Address?

Harry spoke softly and slowly with obvious effort, The Bowery.

The Bowery? Dont you have a permanent mailing address?

He moved his hand in a negative motion. The Bowerys permanent. It aint movin.

Nothing more specific?

He moved his hand slightly.

She smiled and shrugged. Age?

40.

In case of emergency who do you want notified?

I dont really care . . . He smiled slightly, Gallo Brothers.

Gallo Brothers?

He smiled a little broader, Ernest and Julio.

O???? Then she understood and smiled. The winemakers.

Harry blinked his eyes.

She was still smiling, Well, I guess we had better leave that blank. Occupation?

He moved his jaw in a shrugging gesture . . . Dishwasher.

Have you ever been a patient here before?

I dont know.

Dont know?

He shook his head slightly . . . I dont know where I am.

Oh . . . Bellevue.

Nope. He winced as a pain pierced his head, then exhaled sharply, exhausted and tired.

The clerk looked at her form, then at him, I think thats enough for now. You get some rest. She got up to leave.

Do me a favor? See if my coats alright?

She started to say something, then just smiled and nodded, Sure.

Thanks. Harry closed his eyes and slept.

When he awoke he asked the nurse if the clerk had called about his coat.

Coat?

She was going to check to see if its alright.

She probably hasnt had time to yet. Im sure she/ll take care of it.

Harry nodded within himself, unable to really think about it, not sure when he saw the clerk . . . not sure about anything actually. Every now and then there would be a slight glimmer of light, but it would be quickly absorbed by mist and he could not find the energy to really grasp a thought for any length of time and would just drift off into sleep.

Through the following days whenever he was conscious Harry would wonder about his coat and if it was alright, if he was still wearing it when he got here and, if he was, what had happened to it after he got here. Everytime someone came near him he wanted to ask them about his coat, but couldnt seem to summon up the energy. Eventually he felt a couple of days must have passed since he spoke with the clerk, not absolutely certain because he spent so much time sleeping and was still confused about time, but whether it was or not the pressure was building to the point where he had no choice but to ask the nurse again if the clerk had called about his coat.

She frowned agitatedly, What coat?

My coat – Harry could feel himself starting to tremble – remember I asked –

O that. No. Nobody has called about anything.

But she said . . . can you call her?

I dont have time to make calls about coats. I have all I can do right now.

But I have to know. I dont know if – he started to get up, but a sudden pain took his breath away and he fell back on the bed.

Pain in your head?

He could hardly mutter.

The nurse rushed from the room and quickly returned with a hypo and soon the pain subsided and Harry once more drifted off to sleep.

Harry continued to ask about his coat, never being certain if he was asking many times in one day or once in many days, but when the pressure built to the point where he no longer had a choice, he asked, and when he was given an evasive answer he got so upset he usually had to be sedated and another note was made on his chart. Eventually the doctor asked about the notes on his chart and the nurses told him about Harrys preoccupation with his coat and the doctor wrote a request that Harry be interviewed by a psychiatrist, And for krists sake, in the meantime tell him the coats alright.

When a nurse told Harry that his coat was alright he seemed to change instantly, tension draining from his body almost visibly, a hint of color returning to his cheeks. He could feel an endless sigh flow through his body as he drifted back to sleep.

Harry was relaxed, but still a little groggy, when a young psychiatrist visited him one morning. Harry had not been shaved for 3 or 4 days, his head was swathed in bandages that were stained with blood and antiseptics, and he was still wired so his bodily functions could be monitored. The psychiatrist looked at him for a moment, You look depressed.

Harry just blinked.

How do you feel?

Harry shrugged slightly, Okay.

The psychiatrist made a few notes. You seem to be concerned about your clothing.

My coat. I wanted to be sure it was alright.

Were you wearing it when you were admitted?

Harry looked at him for a moment, I dont know.

The psychiatrist made more notes, then looked at Harry. I see. Do you often have lapses of memory?

Harry looked at him, blinking, feeling more and more intimidated. He started sweating. I was unconscious.

The psychiatrist peered at him for a moment, then made another note. Are you often so obsessive about your possessions?

Harry stared, his head shaking slightly, trying earnestly to understand what it was the doctor wanted. He listened hard, and heard the words but he just could not seem to make any sense out of them. They did not seem to have anything to do with him . . . or anything he could think of. Harry did not know what he had done wrong. All Harry could do was look and twist his face into a frown . . .

The psychiatrist stared at Harry then made more notes. Are you always so insecure about your clothing?

Harry could feel himself wilting as the psychiatrist stared at him . . . Eventually he shook his head.

Harrys sweating and trembling increased and he was no longer capable of even trying to understand what the psychiatrist was saying or what it was he wanted. He just stared, on the verge of tears, and shook his head.

The psychiatrist made a final note about the patients hostile and uncooperative behavior and infantile regression, then snapped the metal binder on the chart shut, That will be all. He left.

Harry was still trembling an hour later when a nurse came into the room.

Are you alright?

Harry shook his head slightly.

Youre so pale and sweaty – she touched his forehead – and clammy. Do you have any pain?

He nodded.

Harry continued to tremble many minutes after having been given a hypo, feeling cold and lost, wanting so much to run and hide and just cry . . . cry . . . He looked at the wires going from the various parts of his body to the machinery around the bed knowing that he could disconnect himself easy enough, but he would still be unable to move. He was trapped. He knew his legs would not support him if he tried to stand. And even if he could, he could never find his way to his coat and he could not go anywhere without his coat . . . not now . . . it would be suicide . . . and he did not want to die. Not that way. Not anyway, but especially not that way . . . just a hunk of frozen flesh . . .

He shut his eyes and squeezed them together as hard as possible to shut out the image, then suddenly opened them so his senses could be enveloped by his surroundings and blot out the cold and the stares of the psychiatrist . . . He tried to change his position on the bed, but didnt have much freedom of movement. His eyes got heavy . . . sleepy . . . his body started to feel light . . . the tension slowly started dissolving as the opiate flowed through his body . . . he knew that soon he would fall asleep . . . his body got lighter and lighter . . .

his eyes heavier and heavier . . .

he
could no longer think . . . was only vaguely aware of his body . . . still he felt like he was drowning in tears . . .

Harry Wrights condition continued to improve and soon he was able to walk to the bathroom, at first with assistance, then alone. Another month and he was able to walk around whenever he wanted and spent some time in the t.v. room, when it wasnt too crowded, staying in the back of the room, but spending most of his time playing solitaire or looking at magazines. He was still too weak to do much of anything else and was content to rest and eat, feeling relaxed and secure now that he knew his coat was alright.

He was unable to eat the Thanksgiving dinner, but he did participate energetically in the Christmas festivities, enjoying the food and the entertainments that various organizations presented and the little packages of candy they passed out. He also laughed at their jokes and smiled in recognition of their greetings and MEEEEEEEERY CHRISTMAS.

Now that he was well enough to move around without any ill effects, the first thing he did in the morning was to look out the window and check the weather. The area around the hospital always had a gray, cold look, but he watched the people walking, knowing by the way they moved just how cold it was. He also checked the morning shift and listened to them. Everybody talked about the weather and on the really cold days they were still rubbing their hands together when they got to the ward and hunched their shoulders when they talked about the wind and snow. He watched and listened to the radiators letting out their hiss and smiled . . . .

Even when he got out he/d be warm. He had his coat. He had nothing to worry about, and he would wrap his bathrobe around him and pretend it was his coat and stand by the window and put his nose against the cold glass and feel the heat coming from the radiator . . .

And, from time to time, he would sit, his hands in his bathrobe pockets, thinking about his buddy . . . and how it felt and looked . . . closing his eyes and seeing every inch of his coat, even the black spots from the fire, feeling its weight on his shoulders and the texture of the material against his cheeks and the almost bottomless pockets . . . and he experienced another warmth, the warmth of friendship . . . the warmth of affection.

One morning he was looking at the paper when he recognized the area in a photo, an empty lot on the Bowery. There was a bulldozer in the lot and in front of it were 4 or 5 bodies, ". . . inhabitants of the Bowery who had frozen to death sometime in the past month and were just discovered. They had to be broken loose from the ground with a bulldozer." Harry felt a wave of sickness and panic twist his insides, but then he slowly relaxed as he wrapped his bathrobe around him once again, closed his eyes and affectionately talked with his friend. His friend loved him and would never let that happen to him. He didnt have to worry about that.

Harry had been in the hospital three months and with the return of health and strength came an increased feeling of nervousness. There was a vague tension within him, a gnawing anxiety that grew with each day. He gradually retreated further and further within himself, becoming less communicative and spending more time just sitting with his robe wrapped around him, occasionally going over to the window and staring out at the grayness. It had always been like this, ever since he could remember. The only thing that changed it was drinking. When he had enough to drink things around him seemed to change ... they became friendlier, more comfortable and pleasant and he didnt feel threatened or sickened by what he saw. But the longer he went without drinking the darker things became, the more painful life became ... everything around him became unbearable. It seemed like there was nothing but killing and hurt ... always hurt ... the kind of hurt that stays inside and just keeps growing and gnawing until it takes over everything in you ... always hurt ...

That was why the Bowery was so ideal. In other places when everything got gray and ugly there was always a small part of him that would remember and remind him that it wasnt always like that, that he had actually looked around and liked what he saw ... at times loved it ... loved it with a depth of feeling and involvement, and all he could do was drink to try and re-kindle that feeling of love ... of beauty ... the conflict consuming him.

But the more he drank the more impossible it became to stay, so he had to move on, always feeling the pain of a crying child or a straggly cat, occasionally being brought to tears by the beauty of a flower or a budding tree.

But on the Bowery when he felt that all the beauty had been squeezed from the world and there was nothing but grayness and hurt, he could look around and know he was right because the world he saw was precisely that, and so there was no conflict. The ugliness was real and the wine painted over that and he could go his way, alone, washing dishes, junking, finding some place to nest alone and talk and sing softly to himself and his coat, and drink himself to a state of unconsciousness.

Harrys feeling of anxiety and grief increased with the passing of each day, and so, though it was snowing and cold when they told him all his test results were fine and he would be discharged soon, he was relieved.

Before he was discharged he was visited by the psychiatrist again. He asked Harry what he was going to do when released. More alert than before, he was still confused by the psychiatrist. It seemed that he just could not mean what he said and Harry was trying to understand what it was the psychiatrist wanted. Go home.

The psychiatrist looked at the chart, Wheres that? They dont seem to have it on here.

Harry frowned, The Bowery.

The Bowery? Why would you go there?

I live there.

The psychiatrist made a note. But wouldnt you like to do something better with your life? Like get a good job and be a productive member of society?

Harry shook his head, I work.

The psychiatrist made another note. Washing dishes isnt much of a job.

Harry just looked, trembling slightly inside.

Now that you are free from alcohol you should be able to find a place to live with nicer surroundings.

Harry shook his head, his confusion showing in his expression.

The psychiatrist made a note. Would you like to go some place to rest and get some help in evaluating your – Harry was shaking his head – life and not go back to that old environment?

Harry was still shaking his head, No . . .no, no nut house.

Well now, thats not really – Harry continued shaking his head – the proper way to . . . the psychiatrist looked at Harry intently, disbelief in his expression and voice, Dont you want to better yourself?

Harry stopped shaking his head and stared at the psychiatrist, almost wanting to explain to him that he had found the most comfortable life he had ever had and was going to stay there, but could summon up neither the necessary energy nor the desire. Now at least the psychiatrist was no longer a problem to Harry, the enigma was solved: he was jut another dogooder trying to get involved in someone elses life. Harry stopped frowning and even started to relax slightly . . . . Im fine.

The psychiatrist looked at Harry, exasperated, then slammed the metal binder on the record shut and left.

On the day of his discharge a ward attendant was sent to get Harrys clothing, and Harry started to pace. The tension in his body became more and more acute as he looked at the drab ugliness around him, then out the window at the snow and the trees bending in the wind. He felt the heat from the radiator, then touched his nose to the cold window . . . .

                                                                    then
turned and started pacing again.

After half an hour he went to the nurses station and asked where his clothes were. He was told to relax, that the attendant would be back shortly. He started pacing again, his anxiety and tension becoming so intense he felt brittle, walking from one end of the floor to the other, from time to time looking out the window.

Eventually the charge nurse decided to call and see where the attendant was, assuming he was goldbricking. When she spoke to the clerk in the clothing room she was told that the attendant was still there, that Mr. Wrights clothing could not be found but they were still looking. Well, you tell Walter to come back to the ward and when you find his clothing give us a call. Ward B3W.

Harry caught bits of the tail end of the conversation, Whats that? Cant they find my coat?

They seem to be having some difficulty Mr. Wright, but –

The color instantly drained from Harrys face and his legs weakened, Ive got to have my coat. He leaned against the counter in the nurses station. I got to have my coat!

Just relax Mr. Wright. Dont upset yourself.

Harry was trembling and staring at them, Wheres the clothing room? I/ll find it. Where do they keep the –

Mr. Wright – spoken authoratitively – you must relax or youll have a relapse and –

Just tell me where the room is. I/ll find my coat. I/ll find it . . . Harry was clinging desperately to the counter, feeling weaker by the second, the room starting to spin, his vision blurring . . . he could no longer feel his feet or legs. He started to sag, semi-conscious and sobbing almost incoherently as he relived his long fight to save his coat, feeling the death-like emptiness of separation from the most valuable thing in his life, a friend that was at least as valuable as his life itself . . .

He pulled himself to his feet and pleaded with them to tell him where the clothes room was, I can find my coat . . . I know I can . . . I can find it anywhere . . . I –

Mr. Wright please, you must con –

Walter returned from the clothes room, dropping the clothes receipt on the counter, They cant find his clothes anywhere, Miss Wilson.

Let me look, I can find it . . . and Harry continued to plead and tremble and cling desperately to the counter as a nurse tried to quiet him.

Miss Wilson glanced at the papers quickly then asked Walter what name the clerk had looked under?

Whatever names on there I guess.

She showed him the admission sheet, He was a John Doe when he was admitted. See, theres also an I.D. number. Mr. Wright, what sort of clothing did you have?

A big army coat. I can find it in a minute . . .

Miss Wilson called the clothing room and told them what to look for, and what name and number.

It seemed like forever to Harry as he remained suspended between life and death, the only thing proving to him that he was alive was the curious pain twisting and clawing within him, but in just a few minutes Walter was back with Harrys clothes. They had been sterilized, but they still looked and smelled funky and Walter carried them at arms length from him and wrinkled his nose. Harry grabbed his clothes and hugged them to him, almost crying, and rushed to the mens room to get dressed. He sat on a commode half laughing, half crying, hugging and cradling his coat, telling it how much he loved it and had been waiting for it and he would not have let them keep him away that he didnt have to worry that no matter what happened he would have found him ... rocking back and forth, tears rolling down his cheeks, sobbing and laughing with relief ...

Harry started down the hospital steps when a gust of wind blew snow in his face and momentarily blinded him. He grabbed the hand rail, feeling the cold metal on his hand and the wind biting his face. He pulled his watch cap down around his ears and yanked the large collar of his great coat up around his head and nestled deep into his coat like a butterfly in a cocoon and smiled from deep inside himself. He could feel the cold on his nose and the warmth of his body. His coat was even warmer than he remembered. His lovely and wonderful coat.

The wind stopped and he went down the stairs, holding the railing, the ground slippery and treacherous. When he reached the bottom he shoved his cold hands in his pockets and looked around. There were large snow banks on the sides of the street, its gray filth showing through the whiteness of the newly fallen snow. He started walking cautiously, over the patches of ice everywhere, feeling his body moving inside his coat, hearing the wind and feeling the snow and laughing at them.

He walked carefully down the street to the first liquor store and bought a pint of muscatel. As soon as he got outside he took a drink, standing still long enough to experience it going down and through his body, knowing soon the drabness and ugliness would be tolerable. He put the bottle in his pocket and started walking toward the bus stop. Soon he would be back on the Bowery and he would find a nice deserted building to nest in and leisurely drink his wine, then softly talk and sing to himself and his coat.

He stood with the wind at his back, cuddled in the warmth of his coat, his entire being happy and glowing. He rubbed his cheek against the collar, its roughness reassuring him. They were together. They could take anything together ... do anything together ... survive anything together ... He loved his coat ... and his coat loved him ... and they were together. That was the important thing. No one ... nothing could separate them. And as long as they were together theyd make it. Yeah ... theyd make it ...

The bus came and he hopped aboard and Harry Wright headed home. He was warm ... He was safe ...

The Musician

The Musician

Harold got out of bed at 7am, a few minutes before the alarm was set to sound, put on his slippers, his robe and went to the bathroom. He thought briefly of telling Virginia that he would not have soft boiled eggs for breakfast, but dismissed the thought almost before it formed. He brushed his teeth, then hung his robe on the hanger behind the door, put his pajamas in the hamper, then, after carefully adjusting the water temperature with minute turns of the valves, stepped into the shower stall. When he finished he rubbed himself briskly, put on his robe and shaved. He then combed and brushed his hair neatly into place, then dressed, except for his tie and jacket.

When he got to the kitchen his sisters and his eggs were waiting, Virginia pouring his coffee, Helen, of course, feeding puss, her floor-length robe wrapped tightly around her thinness. Good morning Harold, have a good sleep?

Yes Virginia, I did. How about you?

She nodded, O fine, thank you.

The radio was tuned to a news station and they all listened dutifully to the complete weather report and forecast. When it was over Helen sat down. Well, it sounds like its going to be a nice day.

Harold was in the process of returning his cup to its saucer, Thats good to hear. How did you sleep, Helen?

O, fair to middlin. You know, my back ...

Virginia and Harold nodded and Virginia looked at Harold.

Yes I know. Maybe you should see Dr. Winslow? Virginia nodded and looked at Helen.

Maybe I will if it doesnt let up soon.

Harold listened to his toast crunching, transposing it into the beat of a metronome. When he finally swallowed he took another drink of coffee. Virginia smiled, What will you be playing tonight Harold?

He looked at his sister for a moment, I thought maybe a Beethoven sonata.

O, that would be splendid. Dont you agree, Helen?

Helen thought for a moment, as was expected of her position of being the oldest. Yes I think so. Be sure to dust the piano, Virginia.

O, of course, she smiled at both of them, Its the first thing I do each morning.

Well, I must get to my African violets, and Helen stood and left the kitchen.

And I must be getting to the office. Harold dabbed his lips with his napkin then went back to his rooms to finish dressing. The old house suited their needs admirably, each having a suite of rooms, Harolds upstairs, the ladies downstairs. And too, each had been born in the house and lived their lives there, Helen 71 years, Virginia 67 years, and Harold 53 years. A lifetime.

Harold inspected his jacket for traces of lint, then finished dressing before going down stairs, stairs that at one time, many, many years past, he would run and jump down, or even slide down the banister once or twice maybe, until mother stopped him and from then properly decended the stairs. By the time he got back downstairs Helen had finished with the African violets and had picked up puss/s bowls. Cats are nice, but a house must be kept tidy. Harold put on his hat and though it was a clear and sunny day, with a forecast of temperatures in the seventies, Harold put on his raincoat just in case.

Dont forget your briefcase, Harold, and Virginia handed it to him.

I wouldnt, Virginia. He took the briefcase and pecked her on the cheek, then Helen, and left the house.

He noted, without realizing, the cracks in the sidewalk, noting the difference between now and 5 years ago, 10 years ago, and now and many years ago. At one time they were counted with childish fascination, but that too passed as did the running up and down the stairs. Just as did the desire to be a concert pianist. Mother would not hear of that either . . .

Dad had been dead for many years by then . . . or at least it seemed like many years, having been very young when dad passed away. Some things were precisely etched in the rock of his memory and others were vague . . . just vague . . .

No, mother would not approve of that either. Playing the piano was not for a man, just as running up and down stairs or counting the cracks in the pavement was not for a boy. The law was for a man. Lawyers were men of substance. And after passing the bar mother allowed him a piano and he took lessons. She even listened to him later on. A little bit . . .

He walked up the street noticing the bursting green of the trees and felt a smile floating through him. It took 7 minutes to walk to the subway station, a few seconds to buy a paper, and then down to the platform.

When he got on the train he put his briefcase between his feet and read his paper. He was always nervous about the briefcase and worried that someone might trip over it. From time to time he could feel himself blush when he accidentally tapped someone with it. He had never wanted to carry a briefcase. He did not carry work home. He never had that much responsiblity. But he had to admit that mother was right, it did seem to create an air of prestige. But still, it was an annoyance at times.

He nodded and smiled at his fellow employees and walked through the rooms to his office. He hung up his hat and coat and sat at his desk and looked at his calendar. It was Monday and he could call today. Not now. Later. And perhaps he would say a little more to her today, after all, there really was not a valid reason for only saying hello, how are you? and then, goodbye, have a nice day. Well, we/ll see what happens. For now, work. He took a file from the neat pile on the left corner of his desk and studiously went through each page, making notes, then evaluated the problem, made a few more notes, then reviewed everything again, briefly noting what he thought should be done, and then thought again for a few minutes, tapping the tips of his fingers together, reviewed his notes carefully and thoroughly, then dictated a detailed memo and letter, and when he finished he attached the dictation belt to the file and carefully placed it on top of the neat pile of folders on the right hand side of his desk, which was closest to the door so his secretary could get them more readily. He sat back for a moment, brushed a few bits of paper dust from his desk, then picked up the phone and dialed a number. He listened to it ringing, wetting his lips slightly, and after the second ring he adjusted himself in his chair, waiting expectantly for her voice. He listened for a second then said, Hello. He continued listening, smiling, nodding his head, moving his body ever so slightly as if listening to a piece of music. When he replaced the phone on the cradle he continued to smile and leaned back in his chair, his elbows resting on the arms, hands in front of his face, tapping his finger tips together. Her voice was so lovely. He could still hear it floating to join all those final notes of arias . . .

He remembered the first time he had heard Renata Tebaldi. He had not expected it. He had just turned on the radio and heard a voice that forced him to sit down, immediately, and listen and thrill to the exquisite tones, the incredible artistry . . . O, it was so exciting, just he alone in his rooms, making such a divine discovery. And then, shortly after that evening, he saw her sing Mimi. She was so gorgeous, her voice so sublime. Tremors of excitement still tingled within him when he remembered that evening. And though it was a bitter cold night he waited at the stage door for her and when she finally came out and greeted her group of admirers – no! worshippers – he almost swooned she was so devestatingly beautiful, everything about her shimmered . . . her black hair, her incredible mink coat, her skin, her jewelry and her eyes . . . O those eyes . . . he stared and stared and was so transfixed that he almost forgot to ask for her autograph . . . and the smile when she took the pen and program . . . O, what a rapturous smile . . . .

He leaned back in his chair, eyes closed, hands clasped, sighed almost inaudibly, then slowly opened his eyes and looked at the phone, leaning foreward slightly. Perhaps he would call again later and say a little more to her, just a few words perhaps. He brushed a few more pieces of paper dust from his desk and took the next file from the pile on the left.

At noontime he finished making notes on the file he was reviewing and left for lunch. He looked out the window, first at the people in the street, then up at the cloudless sky, and decided to leave his coat in the office and just wear his suit jacket and hat.

The restaurant was elegant and quiet and he smiled diffidently when he handed the check girl his hat. The Maitre'd bowed, Good afternoon Mr. Livingston. Im afraid your usual table is occupied, but I can give you another close by. Harold smiled, That will be fine. Harold sat and the waiter came over immediately, Good afternoon sir. Harold smiled and nodded properly. Will you have the special sir? Yes, I think I will have the duckling, thank you. And a tomato juice cocktail sir? Yes, please.

Harold sipped his tomato juice and looked around surreptitiously, vaguely wondering what the drinks tasted like that were being served. He did not care for cocktails, but he thought he might, just might, have a martini sometime, but the thought was fleeting and tenuous.

He enjoyed his lunch and briefly wondered how many different waiters had served him since he had been coming here???? My goodness, there really wouldnt be any way of knowing. Or Maitre'ds or hat check girls or washroom attendants or boot blacks or . . . he smiled and chuckled inwardly, or even how many ducklings. Maybe tomorrow he would try to . . . Hmmm, tomorrow . . . stuffed veal chops . . . Just might be able to, you know. Only been on the menu a few years. He brushed his lips lightly with the napkin one last time, then got up and left the restaurant.

He stood just outside the door for a moment, then slowly edged into the lunch-hour crowd and walked to a nearby department store. He browsed quickly in the racks of ties then went to the lingerie department and walked slowly around the display cases looking at the many items on the countertops, in the cases, and especially on the manikins. A few times he brushed his hand against the sheer softness of the garments and allowed his body to give voice to a slight tingle of excitement. He continued strolling through the department for a few more minutes, then left and returned to his office.

He worked on a few more files until about four oclock when he called again. There was that delicious feeling of anticipation as the second ring faded and he heard the click that meant that he would be hearing her voice: Hello, this is the recorded information line for the Stuyvesant Museum. If you are calling for other than General Information, please call – He leaned forward, his elbows resting on his desk – the new sculpture garden is now open during regular museum hours. In it are works by 19th and 20th century American and European artists. In the Willnymer Gallery there is a special showing of 14th and 15th century Japanese prints, now through the end of the month. The exhibition consists – he was smiling as he listened and gently brushed his cheek with the fingertips of his right hand, allowing her voice to flow through him in gentle, soothing currents that made his body feel unaccustomedly alive with an unknown energy – program of lectures, music and dance recitals are scheduled for the evenings. Tonight is a performance of traditional Indian dances related to Shiva. Tomorrow the Bartholemew Quartet will play the music of Handel, Beethoven, and Bartok, while on – His smile broadened, Yes, I think thats wonderful, and he felt a slight flush at hearing himself, and was silent again as he did not want to miss too much of her voice – for ticket information call the museum ticket office. Admission to the Dunbar Gallery is always free where fine paintings, sculptures, graphics – he nodded his head and closed his eyes as little dots of light flashed by and images flowed through his body.

He was still brushing his cheek and smiling when he told her her voice was beautiful, then quickly silenced so he could listen – If you have missed any part of this recording – Her voice blended in with the music it created within him and he felt it as well as heard it and his body once again moved in time to it – Thank you for calling the Stuyvesant Museum and have a nice day. He did not hear the click, he was still experiencing the music . . .

He replaced the phone and continued to keep his eyes closed until the music started to ebb, then he opened them and leaned back in his chair and sighed almost inaudibly as his minds eye watched the music drift away . . .

then he looked at the phone, Have a nice day. He breathed deeply and took another file from the pile on the left side of his desk.

At five oclock he closed the file he was working on, brushed the paper dust off his desk, put his pencils and pens in their proper place, and did the same with everything else, centering his calendar just so, and put the morning paper in his briefcase before leaving.

He read the evening paper on the way home, and when he arrived he hung up his coat, put away his hat, and gave Virginia the morning paper. She loved to read the bridge game and work the crossword puzzle. Thank you, Harold.

Youre quite welcome, Virginia, and he pecked her on the cheek. Then he pecked Helen. How did everything go today?

Fine, Harold. How was your duckling?

O, it was good.

Not too salty?

No, no, as a matter of fact it was just right.

O, I am happy to hear that. You have to be careful with duckling, you know. Very greasy.

Yes, I know. But it was rendered properly. He started upstairs to his rooms.

Dinner will be ready in half an hour, Harold.

Fine, Helen.

We/re having a little change tonight.

O?

Yes. We're having peas and carrots with the lamb rather than cauliflower.

O, good. Good, and he continued up the stairs. He hung up his jacket and turned on his phonograph and put on a recording of arias sung by Renata Tebaldi. As he listened he looked through his carefully filed collection of autographed pictures of opera stars and took out his favorite of her and glanced at it from time to time, hearing his Monday voice blending in an extraordinary way with Tebaldi ... O, how he loved Monday nights. The music of her voice was still with him, and the exquisite magic of Tebaldi, both carressing him as he sat in his chair, all those glorious dreams of music flowing from his soul through his hands as the poets voice read lyrics that invited him to find the melody to clothe them, and he breathed deeply as the experience of those memories was once more reawakened, not to be re-imagined, as the images had long since been distilled and annihilated, but their memory was still there ... the imagined joys were still there ... the ecstasies were still there ... hidden away in the warm folds of his brain where they could never be destroyed by any hand, and though the once brilliant images of concert halls and applause were now only flashes of light passing by his closed eyes, the experience, O, God, the tingle of the experience breathed itself eternally in his soul and he held Tebaldis picture in his hand, his attitude and all his being a prayer of thanks to her and the music and his Monday voice as he listened with his heart ...

At dinner each reviewed their day and they smiled and chatted pleasantly, each trying to make the others happy. Virginia was almost shaking with excitement as she related to Harold what had happened at the supermarket. It was just about the most frightening thing that has ever happened to me.

Really? What was it?

She smiled at Helen, I have already told Helen, but I was checking the eggs – to make certain they werent cracked you know – Harold nodded – when all of a sudden there was the most terrible explosion – Helen started to giggle – it really was you know, Helen. I know dear, Im sorry. Harold smiled and looked at them, but said nothing. Well, there was this terribly dreadful explosion and I dropped the carton of eggs – in the case so no damage was done, thank goodness – but I was trembling so badly I could not move. Finally, after what seemed ages, a clerk came by and I asked him what had happened – I thought there were gangsters trying to rob the store – and he told me someone had dropped a seltzer bottle – Helen started giggling again and Harold smiled then chuckled and Virginia grinned, I know it seems silly now, but I was absolutely terrified. And then, to top it off, I forgot the eggs, and she started giggling too.

After dinner they continued chatting as they drank coffee. Eventually Helen asked Harold if he was ready. Yes, I think so.

Good.

O good. The table was cleared and the dishes set to soak while they went to the parlor. Harold sat at the piano and rubbed his hands for a few minutes, played a few scales, then turned to his sisters, shall I play the Appassionata?

O yes, do.

That would be wonderful, Harold.

He turned to the piano, straightened his back and looked at the keyboard for a moment, then started playing. With the first contact of his fingers with the keys he felt transformed and transported. It was not just that he was no longer Harold Livingston age 53, bachelor, lawyer, living with his two unmarried sisters; or that he transcended his daily life and was now a concert pianist. He transcended even that. He simply became a part of the music. But not a part of the music he played, but the music Beethoven wrote. Many times, through the many years, Harold tried to believe he was hearing something other than what he was playing, but his ear was too keen. There certainly was passion in his playing. And power. And the arpeggios were clear and distinct. He knew his playing was inspired and he had great respect for the music, but he also knew that there was a slight stiffness and imperfection of technique. But what he did not hear was of even greater importance than what he did, for he did not hear the brilliance of imagination, that rush of genius that made for greatness which was the only flaw that practice could not erase . . . not now. But Harold had long since stopped hearing the notes coming from the piano and listened instead to the music that came from his heart, the music that was in the soul of the notes. This is what Harold heard as he watched his fingers moving across the keyboard, and what flowed through his being . . .

When he finished he sat still for a moment, still experiencing the music, then smiled and turned and looked at his applauding sisters who were thrilled beyond words, having heard the greatest rendition of the Appassionata ever performed. He stood and bowed and walked over to his sisters. Thank you. Thank you.

O it was marvellous, Harold, simply marvellous.

O yes, it was the finest I have ever heard.

I'll go make some hot chocolate for us to have with our cake. O, how I love Monday nights.

Before retiring Harold played the Sviatoslav Richter recording of the Appassionata, his eyes closed, elbows resting on the arms of his chair, hands in front of his face, fingertips touching slightly. He heard the music . . . From time to time he smiled and nodded his head in approval, feeling a sensation of wholeness as the music within him matched the music without. When the music stopped he continued sitting for many minutes with his eyes closed until the flashing lights vanished. He got up and put the record carefully in its jacket. Virginia is quite right about Monday, though it is not just the night that is wonderful.

He undressed and hung everything in its proper place, put on his pajamas and robe and went to the bathroom and brushed his teeth, then rinsed his mouth. He looked in the mirror, then turned off the light and went back to his bedroom. He lay on his back for a few moments feeling the silence, then thought that perhaps he would not have boiled eggs for breakfast . . . but he did not have to make that decision now. He turned on his side, closed his eyes, and slept.

Of Whales and Dreams

Many, many years ago a man told me that to deny my dream was to sell my soul. I was young and did not know that the words were finding their own particular place within me so they would be mine forever, but I do remember blinking my eyes and nodding my head as if the very motion was forcing the truth in what he said deeper within me.

And I was full of dreams. Dreams, dreams, dreams. And I dream still.

And the whale is a dream.

When I was a child and landlocked, playing ships was my game. A stick in water was fine. I did not need sails or steam, only imagination, and my ships sailed through mirror-like waters or weathered the most treacherous of storms. And the suns reflection looked up at me from the south sea lagoons, or, as a breeze rippled the water, the reflection became a broken moon in the Atlantic. And sea-walls and jetties were my playgrounds and I would spend endless days on the shore or pier watching the various vessels of every description and flag sail in and out of the harbor, or drop their anchor and rest while small launches brought men ashore. I was aware the pilots knew just where each ship should be, and how much room to leave, yet still I constantly marvelled at how a harbor filled with anchored ships could be so free of problems. And I would sit for hours watching the tide slowly change the positions of the ships as they tugged at their anchor chains. I watched and dreamed.

And then, as the years went so slowly by, I would stand at the head of a pier and wait for a tug to tie up, hoping the captain would see me and yell down for me to come aboard, that they needed a messboy, and I would leap on her deck and the mooring lines would be let go immediately and we would be off on our adventure.

And at night I would lie in my bed and allow my imagination to take me any-which-where and I would sail to the places I had seen in pictures, and see our tug battling the seas of Cape Hatteras, or sailing thru the Keys, the very words sounding distant and romantic.

And one day I did leap on a tug and crossed the harbor and back. I was living in a dream. An old deckhand chuckled at me and told me about his days at sea and all the countries he had seen and all the oceans he had crossed, and told me of the time he shipped on a whaler and how the whales looked as they flowed through the sea, and of the sudden bursting forth when they breached and the banging roar of the huge flukes cracking the surface of the water. And he even imitated the voice of a whale. The captain let me in the wheel house, and allowed me to take the wheel for a minute, but I spent almost all of those few hours with the old deckhand listening to more and more stories about whales. For days and nights I relived that day, dreaming always of teaching the whales to dance.

While still in my mid-teens I finally went to sea. A lifetime spent dreaming of the sea died and now a new life of living the dream had begun. And still I pursued my dream even though it was now my life. I never did ship on a whaler, but manys the time Ive seen them break the surface of the sea, barely causing a ripple, looking so gentle and strong and indomitable, and, as I stood at the gunnel watching them, in my head I would be playing a song on a concertina and pipe, teaching them to dance, and they honked their glee as they whirled and twirled through the water waving their flukes in time and merriment to the music . . .

And when it came time to stop they sang a final note and waved and continued on their inevitable way, and me on mine, leaning against the gunnel, staring at the disappearing ripples, feeling a part of them was still with me and a part of me with them. They somehow became a part of my dream, in some strange way as important a part of the dream as me. It took the two of us to make the dream. And it does still.

And still I dream though Ive been on the beach now for some years, in Snug Harbor. We/re all ex-sailors here and talk of the many ports we/ve been to, of the endless countries and people we/ve seen, so many of which have changed names a dozen times over. But I spend as much time alone as possible, looking down at the harbor, a harbor that was once filled with vessels of every type, a harbor that is now spotted with an occasional ship. As with all things its changed.

But my dreams the same. And I pursue it still.

Ive sailed so long and sewn so much canvas that the tips of my fingers are blunted and hard, and hauled so many ropes my hands are as rough as manilla hemp; Ive scampered up ratlins in heavy seas and sat on the hatch of a brand new freighter feeling the thump of her engine. Memories . . . all memories. Images to help pass a day. But only for a short time. I chase them with my dream . . . my vision. I close my eyes and hear the music and they come, all about me, dancing and singing and O how lovely it is to see the sea rolling from their backs that shine and glisten and though theyre monstrous in size they barely send out a ripple as they go through endless seas. And I call to them, through cupped hands, with a loud and happy, HELLO MY FRIENDS . . . and they wave their flukes at me and we dance and laugh and this thing called death no longer exists, being dissolved in our oneness, and I know that so long as my heart, and that timeless, ageless leviathan part of me, is filled with my dream . . . my vision of dancing with my friends . . . that there is only life, life as large and strong and beautiful and full of gentleness and joy as my friends, and where they go I go also, and we are inseparable, and my life is theirs and theirs mine, and we are all part of the same dream.

Song of the Silent Snow

He tried to judge the weather by the light easing through his eyelids, a gray bordering on black. Perhaps he was wrong, maybe it wasnt almost time for the alarm to go off. Maybe the pills affected his sense of time too – no, that wasnt it, he could definitely sense that it was close to 7. Must be cloudy and overcast, or maybe it even snowed like predicted. Could be. Might even be snowing now. He felt his face wrinkle into a squint as he strained to hear the snow ... or rain if it had gotten suddenly warmer ... but heard nothing. Not even a hint of wind.

He concentrated on the tip of his nose, but it didnt feel so cold. That didnt necessarily mean anything. There were many mornings when he awoke and his nose wasnt cold. Actually, now that he thought about it, it very seldom was in the morning. It was in the middle of the night that it got cold and sometimes kept him awake. I guess thats one good thing about those pills, dont have to get up in the middle of the night to go to the bathroom. Thats what used to start it off, getting up and by the time he was back under the covers his nose was cold and he just could not seem to get back to sleep and would lie there, half awake and half asleep, never knowing if he was dreaming or thinking, knowing the alarm would be ringing sooner or later and dreading it, wishing he could get back to sleep but his nose was so cold it hurt, and he would fight hard against the coldness, and his sleeplessness, and lay there anticipating the alarms sudden clanging, but never totally prepared for its attack, and when it finally did thrust itself upon him, his body shaking in reaction, he felt he could sleep forever if he just shut his eyes . . . and so he would lie there fighting to relax and sleep, think of the hour he went to bed and the approximate time he fell asleep, calculating how much sleep he had, and how much he might get, total, and how much he should get in order to do a good days work. Above all he wanted . . . no, it was imperative that he be more than sufficient for the demands of his work . . . especially now that they had moved to the suburbs and assumed the responsibility of owning a house. It brought with it advantages, but also many changes. It used to be a 15 minute ride to work, and then a short walk. But now it was almost that long to get to the station, and then it was another hour to Grand Central, providing there werent any delays, and thank God there usually werent. Thats one of the reasons they decided on Connecticut rather than Long Island. All in all he had to get up almost 2 hours earlier than when they lived in New York City. But that had been anticipated. What was unexpected was his lying awake counting those hours, trying desperately to get more rest, but the harder he tried the more firmly he remained entrapped in that strange area between sleep and wakefulness, from time to time falling fitfully into one then the other, literally feeling himself bouncing off their unseen walls until he dragged himself out of the bed and forced himself into another day.

But time was only one element of the night that twisted itself into his consciousness. When he tried to clear his mind and just relax he thought of the sudden, and huge, drop in their bank balance when they made the down-payment on the house. He had carefully reviewed the entire matter with his accountant, before buying the house, and the purchase price was not only well within their means, but because of the tax writeoffs his net cost would not be more than when he was paying rent, and with no equity. Yes, that was the phrase he latched on to during those mornings, he was building an equity and in these days of uncertainty that was vitally important. He had gone over it many times and there was never the slightest doubt about the money, except when he lay awake in the middle of the night trying desperately to get back to sleep and get the proper rest before the alarm went off.

And so he would think of the house, the house that gave them so much more room and allowed the kids to run and jump without worrying about disturbing anyone under them. And Alice had the kitchen she wanted, with ample room for hanging pots and pans and whatever else she wanted to hang from a rack or nail. And, of course, there was the joy of decorating your own home, feeling completely free to make any changes you want, and ten thousand other advantages, and so he thought of all those things and the financial concerns would dissipate, and eventually he would feel himself sliding into sleep, but for some reason a part of him seemed to cling, ever so lightly, to a thin thread of wakefulness and so when the alarm suddenly startled him he was not dragged from a deep state of rest, but more or less jolted from its nearest edge with a sharp twist of exhaustive nausea and a foul thickness in his mouth.

But since coming home from the hospital the tranquillizers and the sleeping pill prevented his being awakened and so all those thoughts, worries and concerns no longer assaulted him during the night. He still awoke shortly before the alarm went off, but it went off much later now that he wasnt going to the office, and though his body was sluggish from the drugs, and his mouth thick and foul tasting, he did not have to battle that nervous exhaustion that the doctors said was resposible for his breakdown. But there was still this time of anticipation and dread.

He lay as still as possible, breathing quietly, listening intently to see if there had been any noticeable change, but there wasnt. He still heard nothing and it wasnt any brighter. He sensed Alice was awake too, but said nothing, though he wanted to turn over and just touch her gently and thank her for being there, for loving him, but the inertia from the drugs was impossible to overcome and so he lay still, breathing quietly, and trying not to think about the fact that there was another day to face ...

But it was not just the drugs that made it impossible for him to turn and touch his wife and reassure her and tell her that he loved her and appreciated everything; it was the responsibility that accompanies such a gesture. If it were possible to just touch her in that way that she understood so well, if he were to place his hand gently on her cheek and let his feeling of love flow to her as he had so often in the past, she would turn and smile and hold his hand and kiss it and he knew he was now unable to contend with that, that he would be forced to hunt for words or expressions and none were available to him. He was suddenly so overwhelmed by the responsiblity of love ... the responsibility of living. And so he lay on his side facing away from his wife, breathing quietly, eyes closed against the day, waiting for the alarm to ring and when it did he knew Alice would stop it immediately, not wanting it to awaken him, and get out of bed as gently as possible so she would not disturb him. If only he could let her know that she did not have to leap at the clock and then slide from the bed and tiptoe into the bathroom, quietly closing the door, turning the water on to a bare trickle, splashing the sleep from her eyes, not bathing until he was awake and up ... he listening to her almost inaudible movements, wishing he could say its alright, that she could take her shower now, and that she did not have to keep the kids so quiet while they ate and got ready for school ... but he shuddered at the thought.

Maybe soon he could stop taking those pills. Maybe soon he could just get up and go downstairs and have breakfast with his family. Maybe soon he would be going to his office like he used to. Maybe soon he could just put his arms around his wife and simply say, I love you, without fear or guilt or worrying about what he would say after. The major problem was simply that he could not find anything positive or healthy to focus his mind on. If he thought about his work he only experienced worry and concern: was he still capable of performing effectively? will he have a job when he got well? or should he say, if he got well? No, no, he had to get well. But what was wrong with him? He did not really know. He had talked with the people in the hospital and spent time with Dr. Richter, but he still did not know what was wrong with him. What the hell did nervous exhaustion mean?

What did rest mean? Was this rest? Was this going to get him well? Well from what???? O God! He had to get away from that. But if he thought about his wife and children such a sadness flowed through him that he wanted to cry and yet he did not know why. What was there to cry about? He loved them. They loved him. No one was dying, so why cry? Or was he dying? Were there certain types of death he knew nothing about? Was it possible to stay like this forever? Locked into these thoughts in a futile attempt to avoid his feelings? But even if the lock is opened where could he go? When he battled his way free he always ended up in the same place, engulfed by those feelings that literally froze his body and made him shudder with unknown fears and dread, that made the misery of the previous thoughts almost seem like a pleasure. And so he went from a painful level to one that was unbearable, unable to free himself from the process, listening to the sound of another morning as the children scuttled around, continually being hushed by Alice, dressing, eating, gathering books, suddenly remembering something important and eventually rushing from the house.

He continued to lay immobile, eyes shut, until the need to urinate forced him from the bed and he went to the bathroom. He ignored the mirror and washed quickly and dressed in old clothes. He pulled the window shade aside a few inches and looked out ... He relaxed a trifle and his face started slipping into a smile as he watched the snow falling straight down, an inch or so on the ground, the trees and bushes covered. The entire front yard white and glistening, the whiteness of the yard sectioned by the footprints of Beth and Michael. A semblance of joy started awakening within him as he looked at the quiet scene – a Cardinal and his lady suddenly splitting the whiteness – remembering sleighriding ... and then a pain stabbed him as he realized that the children should have been hooting and hollering at seeing the snow but were undoubtedly told to be quiet, that daddy is sleeping and needs his rest. He stared out the window, aware of the hazards of snow on the roads, and the fact that the driveway would have to be shoveled and ...

he escaped

down the stairs slowly.

Alice was sitting at the table, drinking coffee. She started smiling as soon as she heard Harry coming down the stairs. Have a good sleep, sweetheart?

Harry shrugged and nodded, Yeah.

Its snowing. Isnt it beautiful?

He nodded again and went to the stove to pour himself a cup of coffee. Alice got up. Here, let me do that, honey. You sit down.

No, no, thats alright. I can get it. Alice stopped half way to the stove, You sure? Its no trouble. Harry was trying to smile but kept frowning. Please, please, its alright.

Alice stood still for a moment, watching, sensing his irritation, then attempting again. Can I get you something to eat? Toast? Biscuits?

No, no. Just sit down, Alice. *Please*. He carefully carried his cup to the table and sat.

Alice followed him and sat down slowly not wanting to shake the table and spill his coffee. They both looked out the window at the falling snow. Alice snapped into another smile. Michael was barely dressed when he went out to test the snow. He made a snowball and threw it and came back in all beaming and saying its great packing and the sleighriding will be terrific. Im certainly happy this is Friday. And so are they. This could well be the last snow of the season.

Harry looked at her, his face relaxed, almost smiling, Thats right, isnt it? Its the middle of March.

Thats right, and we survived our first winter in Connecticut without frostbite.

Its not exactly the wilderness.

No. But it is a lot different than the city. Its so incredibly beautiful. Her face beamed and radiated. O Harry, Im so happy we moved here. Thank you for the house and the trees, and . . . and everything.

Harry looked at her for a moment as she looked at him lovingly, then nodded and finished his coffee and got up. Guess I/d better get going.

Going for a walk?

Yes.

Do you think its a good idea to go walking now? I mean, it looks awfully slippery and treacherous.

Its the only thing Im doing to get well, I –

That isnt true darling – her voice filled with warmth and affection – youre doing everything you can.

Harry was nodding his head, Yes, I suppose so, but it doesnt seem like much to me.

She touched his arm tentatively, then took a hand in both of hers. Try not to be so hard on yourself. Youre looking better every day.

Harry looked at her and pulled his hand from hers, a feeling of annoyance creeping through him, then conflict and tension, wanting to tell Alice not to be so damned patronizing, but the necessary anger wasnt there to force the words from his mouth. His voice was flat, but it did reflect his irritation. Doctors orders. I walk every day. Strengthen the heart.

Alice stood still as Harry finished dressing, not trusting herself to say anything, afraid she would start yelling or calling him a self-pitying bastard, and just watched, in silence, as he prepared himself for the weather . . . then decided she would try again. Kiss goodbye? leaning forward to kiss him, and be kissed, Harry immediately rigid, turning his cheek to her as he backed away. He looked at her for a brief moment, his expression one of confusion. See you later.

Alice watched him walk across the yard, the only moving object in the snow. He picked his way slowly, and carefully, to the street . . .

She spun around and went to the kitchen and started scrubbing a pan, tightening her jaw, feeling an ache in her hands and arms, scrubbing so hard it was as if she was trying to rub a hole in the pan. She suddenly dropped it in the sink. Goddamn it. Im not going to put up with this nonsense. That Richter had better do something Im going to call him today and – she suddenly sagged over the sink and threw the soap pad at the pan. It was the same old thing. Every time she got angry with Harry she remembered what the doctor said: that it was expected that Harry would be withdrawn for a while, but his condition would improve with time and rest. She looked out the window over the sink at the almost unnatural quietness outside, which increased the turmoil within her. Time. Time, time!!!! It seems like its what everything needs but we never have enough of. Goddam time! You hear me time? Goddamn you! Whose side you on anyway?!

Harry crossed the street to the side that was free of houses. Just trees all the way up the slight incline to the next street. On the other side he could see houses but they were well back and only visible because the trees were bare. He looked up at the large nests in a couple of trees, nests that he had been told were squirrels. He had been surprised to learn that squirrels had nests like those, having always thought they only lived in the hollows of trees as in cartoons. He passed them each day these past weeks, since being released from the hospital, stopping and checking, yet never once did he see a squirrel anywhere near either nest, or any other creature for that matter. Always nothing.

When he first started walking he only walked for ten minutes, slowly, but now he was walking a couple of miles each morning. At first he had to push himself a little to get up the slight hill, but he knew after he reached the top that sooner or later the walking would get easier, his head clearing more and more, and by the time he got back he would be feeling much better than when he left, but still feeling isolated from his family . . . and everything else. He had talked with Dr. Richter about it the last time he saw him, telling him he thought he would feel better if he did not have to take those pills, but the doctor warned him about trying to do too much too soon, so he reluctantly continued to take them, constantly promising himself that he would stop them soon, or at least cut down on the dosage no matter what Richter said. But that was in the future. Right now he just had to put one foot in front of the other and walk along the now familiar streets.

When he got to the top of the hill he stopped for a moment to catch his breath and look around. There was no living creature to be seen. Everything was still. And the falling snow had a sense of stillness about it. It fluttered through the air and fell to the ground or trees or bushes never seeming to be alien to the surroundings, as if it had always been there and was just another part of the air, and everything else that surrounded him. He felt it brush his face as he looked up at the sky, seeing no difference between the air and sky, all a soft gray with a light of its own, the snow floating through the illuminated grayness.

Harry looked at the bare trees as he walked, their limbs auraed with snow, the evergreen trees and bushes flocked and bending slightly from the moist weight of the snow. The stillness was new to him, a quietness never heard of or read about, but one he was now experiencing. And though there was an almost tangible quality about the air it was lighter than ever before and Harry felt a floating sensation soothe him as he walked, there seeming to be less and less resistance to his movement.

He looked down at the street, and the unbroken whiteness, and watched his foot touch the snow and listened to the slight crunching sound as he stepped forward. He looked back at his footprints. They were fascinating. He had been the only one to walk along this street today. There wasnt even the mark of a dog or squirrel, or the scratch of a bird. He continued through the soft, silent snow, a feeling of peace starting to flow through him, helping make his step lighter and easier.

He looked at the houses he had been passing these weeks and though he had never studied them carefully they had become familiar through the process of seeing them so often, and he was now impressed with the change in their appearance as he looked at them through the gray of the air and whiteness of the snow, each house, shrub, tree, bush and mailbox trimmed with snow and blending into the air as if they were just a picture projected upon the still, pearly grayness, just an impression created by the silent snow, a picture on the edge and verge of disappearing and leaving only the air and snow through which he now lightly walked.

He turned another corner noticing the split rail fence, his minds eye filling in a manger scene with animals watching the quiet child while the Wise Men profferred presents and lay them at the feet of Mary and Joseph ...

Jesus, was Christmas only a few months ago? It seems so distant, so distant that he wondered where the memory came from. But its only a week or so until Spring . . . spring . . . yes, it is the last snow of the winter. This will be it. No more. The kids will have to do all their sleighriding this weekend and then put the sleighs away until next winter . . .

Yes, winter *will* come again. But soon it will be spring. But whatever the season will there ever be another day like today, like it is right now? No . . . no . . . No, there can never be another to compare . . . to be absorbed by . . . to become a part of . . .

He continued walking but his pace slowed. He did not want this walk to end. He did not want to think of it ending. He wanted to abandon himself to this experience . . . abandon himself to the soft, illuminated air, and the silent snow that surrounded him, touched him, clung to him, little clumps hanging from his eyebrows, vaguely visible as translucent objects seen from the edge of vision . . .

Vision . . .

It was all a vision. A vision without . . . a vision seen all around him yet experienced within. His lungs functioned easier, his breathing calm and comfortable; his heartbeat relaxed and regular; his legs feeling light and his feet and hands warm . . .

yes warm, and even his nose seemed to be warm, wonderfully warm . . .

yes, all warm and he knew he was smiling and that his smile was warm.

He stopped as he reached the turning point. He had walked a mile. Time to start back. He looked at the nearby homes, the ones in the distance seeming to be almost amorphous as they blended with the illuminated air; then up at the trees, their snow-rimmed grayness disappearing in the light. He saw a crow sitting still near the tip of a limb, its blackness startling. He stared and waited for the call, blinking automatically as the snow brushed his eyes, but not changing the direction of his sight. He stood absolutely still. And quiet. Then he heard the call. Three times. The crow above answered and rose slowly and seemed to hover over the limb, the snow ignoring the beating wings, continuing to fall straight and seeming to flow through the crow as it flew to its mate. He watched until it was out of sight, wondering if that could really have been the first sound he heard since leaving the house, or was it just the first he noticed?

He turned and took the first, slow step back.

He retraced his footsteps, the only footsteps in the snow. They seemed small, and though they were alone they did not seem to be lonely. He smiled at the thought of lonely footprints, as if footprints could have a life of their own, or even that they could reflect the life of their maker. Perhaps . . . who knows? But thats neither here nor there. He was walking amongst his own footprints, simply walking and leaving another set of prints facing in the opposite direction.

And so he walked, keeping himself company. He noticed movement from the corner of his eye and saw two dogs emerging from the trees, snow hanging from their long hair, walking quietly through the snow. They glanced at him briefly and continued on their journey, their noses in turn sniffing at the snow, the trees, the air, but always moving slowly and silently. Harry did not stop, or slacken his pace, as he briefly watched them once again disappear into and behind the trees and shrubs.

He turned another corner and there was a long stretch of flat, crisp whiteness, broken only by his footprints, stretching out in front of him and seeming to disappear in the white/gray distance. It did not seem possible, but the air was even softer and quieter. He continued walking alongside his prints feeling he could walk forever, that as long as the silent snow continued falling he could continue walking, and as he did he would leave behind all worries and cares, all horrors of the past and future. There would be nothing to bother him or torture his mind and fill his body with tremors of fear, the dark night of the soul over.

There would only be himself and the soft, silent snow; and each flake, in its own life, its own separate and distinct entity, would bring with it its own joy, and he would easily partake of that joy as he continued walking, the gentle, silent snow falling ever so quietly, ever so joyously . . .

yes, and ever so love-ing-ly . . .
love-
ing-ly . . . .

Of course! thats why the air is so brightly gray and alive instead of the dismal drabness you would expect. Its the lovingness of the snow. God, how soothing it is.

Yes, he could walk forever. He could so easily continue to walk and all thoughts of death would fall away, absorbed by the silent snow.

Harrys breathing became more and more easy as he walked until he was no longer aware of breathing or even if he was breathing, as if the air was simply passing through him, rejuvenating his body without him having to go through the process of breathing. Soon he no longer heard the crunch of his foot on the snow no matter how he strained to hear it, and it did not surprise him as his body felt so light it seemed impossible for him to even leave a print, all he knew was that he could walk forever.

He approached his street but, instead of turning on to it, he continued walking straight, something drawing him down a street he had never been on before, a street totally strange to him, completely unlike any of the others around him. And as he walked his body continued to feel lighter and lighter as if the sparkle in the silent snow, and the sparkle that illuminated the air, was flowing through him and slowly filled every cell and fiber of his being. He knew that he was glowing. He knew that his eyes were afire with that light. He knew that light shimmered from him even through his clothing. He felt his legs getting lighter and when he looked down there were no footprints. The soft cloth of snow spread over the street was still unstepped upon and as far back as he could see there were no footprints. He turned and looked ahead, feeling his movement through the light of the gray, white air, feeling the light become more and more a part of him as he became more and more a part of the light, and all of his being was filled with incredible joy as the light grew brighter and brighter ...

and

then he heard it, very faintly at first, but distinct just the same. He heard the snow falling gently through the air, each flake sounded distinctly different, yet just as each fell unhindered by another, so their sound did not clash or interfere with each other, but blended into a snow song that he knew very few had ever heard. And that song became louder, though always gentle, as he continued to be absorbed by the light, to become one with the light ... and now there werent any feet to leave prints, or a body or eyes to glow, but just light and sound and pure joy, pure eternal joy. No past, no future, no, not even a present, just ever new joy where there wasnt even a memory of pain or struggle or sorrow ... just ever new joy ...

and he knew

he could stay here forever.

But then the song of the silent snow was slowly replaced with another sound, vague at first but then more and more familiar as he heard it within him. It was a sound he knew, but could not yet identify. It became more distinct and he listened more intently while still trying to cling to the snow song. The new sound gradually absorbed all his attention until it too started to sing within him ... then he finally recognized it, smiling suddenly, and then it was the only song he heard ... the song of Alice and the children, and he re-experienced all the joys of their life together ...

yet still he clung to the thought of the light and the joy of the song of the silent snow, yearning once again to be filled with that joy that forever eliminated doubt and fear, struggling to nurture that fading joy ... but then a new sound stabbed him and he suddenly had to fight for breath as he heard his family crying because of his absense and experienced their pain and sorrow, and was then overwhelmed with the realization that he had to go back home. No matter how sweet the song of the silent snow, how beautiful the light, how exquisite the joy, he had to go home.

As he surrendered to this realization he became vaguely aware of his body. He felt that his eyes were still glowing, but now he could feel his feet on the ground, and as he became increasingly aware of his movements, he also became aware that the crying had ceased and he once again felt the love song of his family within him. He felt his face smile as he listened to their voices and felt the warmth of happiness spread through him. It was not the joy of moments ago, but a happiness he had not known for what seemed many, many years, though his mind told him it had only been months; a happiness that he had felt for many years, a happiness he thought had gone forever.

He heard the crunch of the snow under his feet, but once more felt lighter . . . unrestricted . . . able to move freely through the pearly gray air and silent snow.

He stopped and stood quietly watching and feeling the snow. He turned and looked behind him at the place where his footprints stopped. A part of him yearned to retrace his steps, to once again become a part of the joy he had briefly experienced, but he knew he could not . . . did not . . . want to ignore the other voices within him. He turned and firmly started walking toward home. He did not know what had happened, but whatever it was he knew he now had hope and what once was could be again. He could re-awaken a part of that joy and take home the song of the silent snow. He could share it. He walked a little faster. He knew his eyes were glowing and that Alice would see it. He also knew he could hold her hand.

Selected Grove Press Paperbacks

62372-X	BRECHT, BERTOLT / The Caucasian Chalk Circle / $5.95
17109-8	BRECHT, BERTOLT / The Good Woman of Setzuan / $4.50
17112-8	BRECHT, BERTOLT / Galileo / $4.95
17065-2	BRECHT, BERTOLT / The Mother / $7.95
17106-3	BRECHT, BERTOLT / Mother Courage and Her Children / $3.95
17472-0	BRECHT, BERTOLT / Threepenny Opera / $3.95
17393-7	BRETON ANDRE / Nadja / $6.95
13011-9	BULGAKOV, MIKHAIL / The Master and Margarita / $6.95
17108-X	BURROUGHS, WILLIAM S. / Naked Lunch / $4.95
17749-5	BURROUGHS, WILLIAM S. / The Soft Machine, Nova Express, The Wild Boys: Three Novels / $5.95
62488-2	CLARK, AL, ed. / The Film Year Book 1984 / $12.95
17038-5	CLEARY, THOMAS / The Original Face: An Anthology of Rinzai Zen / $4.95
17735-5	CLEVE, JOHN / The Crusader Books I and II / $5.95
17411-9	CLURMAN, HAROLD (Ed.) / Nine Plays of the Modern Theater (Waiting for Godot by Samuel Beckett, The Visit by Friedrich Durrenmatt, Tango by Slawomir Mrozek, The Caucasian Chalk Circle by Bertolt Brecht, The Balcony by Jean Genet, Rhinoceros by Eugene Ionesco, American Buffalo by David Mamet, The Birthday Party by Harold Pinter, Rosencrantz and Guildenstern Are Dead by Tom Stoppard) / $15.95
17962-5	COHN, RUBY / New American Dramatists: 1960-1980 / $7.95
17971-4	COOVER, ROBERT / Spanking the Maid / $4.95
17535-1	COWARD, NOEL / Three Plays by Noel Coward (Private Lives, Hay Fever, Blithe Spirit) / $7.95
17740-1	CRAFTS, KATHY & HAUTHER, BRENDA / How To Beat the System: The Student's Guide to Good Grades / $3.95
17219-1	CUMMINGS, E.E. / 100 Selected Poems / $5.50
17329-5	DOOLITTLE, HILDA / Selected Poems of H.D. / $9.95
17863-7	DOSS, MARGOT PATTERSON / San Francisco at Your Feet (Second Revised Edition) / $8.95
17398-8	DOYLE, RODGER, & REDDING, JAMES / The Complete Food Handbook (revised any updated edition) / $3.50
17987-0	DURAS, MARGUERITE / Four Novels: The Afternoon of Mr. Andesmas; 10:30 on a Summer Night; Moderato Cantabile; The Square) / $9.95
17246-9	DURRENMATT, FRIEDRICH / The Physicists / $6.95
17239-6	DURRENMATT, FRIEDRICH / The Visit / $5.95
17990-0	FANON, FRANZ / Black Skin, White Masks / $8.95
17327-9	FANON, FRANZ / The Wretched of the Earth / $6.95
17754-1	FAWCETT, ANTHONY / John Lennon: One Day At A Time, A Personal Biography (Revised Edition) / $8.95
17902-1	FEUERSTEIN, GEORG / The Essence of Yoga / $3.95

17278-7	KEROUAC, JACK / Dr. Sax / $5.95
17171-3	KEROUAC, JACK / Lonesome Traveler / $5.95
17287-6	KEROUAC, JACK / Mexico City Blues / $9.95
62173-5	KEROUAC, JACK / Satori in Paris / $4.95
17035-0	KERR, CARMEN / Sex for Women Who Want to Have Fun and Loving Relationships With Equals / $9.95
17981-1	KINGSLEY, PHILIP / The Complete Hair Book: The Ultimate Guide to Your Hair's Health and Beauty / $10.95
62424-6	LAWRENCE, D.H. / Lady Chatterley's Lover / $3.95
17178-0	LESTER, JULIUS / Black Folktales / $5.95
17481-X	LEWIS, MATTHEW / The Monk / $12.50
17391-0	LINSSEN, ROBERT / Living Zen / $12.50
17114-4	MALCOLM X (Breitman., ed.) / Malcolm X Speaks / $6.95
17023-7	MALRAUX, ANDRE/The Conquerors/$3.95
17068-7	MALRAUX, ANDRE/Lazarus/$2.95
17093-8	MALRAUX, ANDRE / Man's Hope / $12.50
17016-4	MAMET, DAVID / American Buffalo / $5.95
62049-6	MAMET, DAVID / Glengarry Glenn Ross / $6.95
17040-7	MAMET, DAVID / A Life in the Theatre / $9.95
17043-1	MAMET, DAVID / Sexual Perversity in Chicago & The Duck Variations / $7.95
17471-2	MILLER, HENRY / Black Spring / $4.95
62375-4	MILLER, HENRY / Tropic of Cancer / $7.95
62379-7	MILLER, HENRY / Tropic of Capricorn / $7.95
17933-1	MROZEK, SLAWOMIR / Three Plays: Striptease, Tango, Vatzlav / $12.50
13035-6	NERUDA, PABLO / Five Decades: Poems 1925-1970. bilingual ed. / $14.50
62243-X	NICOSIA, GERALD / Memory Babe: A Critical Biography of Jack Kerouac / $11.95
17092-X	ODETS, CLIFFORD / Six Plays (Waiting for Lefty, Awake and Sing, Golden Boy, Rocket to the Moon, Till the Day I Die, Paradise Lost) / $7.95
17650-2	OE, KENZABURO / A Personal Matter / $6.95
17002-4	OE, KENZABURO / Teach Us To Outgrow Our Madness (The Day He Himself Shall Wipe My Tears Away; Prize Stock; Teach Us to Outgrow Our Madness; Aghwee The Sky Monster) / $4.95
17992-7	PAZ, OCTAVIO / The Labyrinth of Solitude / $10.95
17084-9	PINTER, HAROLD / Betrayal / $6.95
17232-9	PINTER, HAROLD / The Birthday Party & The Room / $6.95
17251-5	PINTER, HAROLD / The Homecoming / $5.95
17539-5	POMERANCE / The Elephant Man / $5.95
62013-9	PORTWOOD, DORIS / Common Sense Suicide: The Final Right / $8.00

17658-8	REAGE, PAULINE / The Story of O, Part II; Return to the Chateau / $3.95
62169-7	RECHY, JOHN / City of Night / $4.50
62171-9	RECHY, JOHN / Numbers / $8.95
13017-8	ROBBE-GRILLET, ALAIN / (Djinn and La Maison de Rendez-Vous) / $8.95
62423-8	ROBBE—GRILLET, ALAIN / For a New Novel: Essays on Fiction / $9.95
17117-9	ROBBE-GRILLET, ALAIN / The Voyeur / 6.95
17490-9	ROSSET, BARNEY, ed. / Evergreen Review Reader: 1962-1967 / $12.50
62498-X	ROSSET, PETER and VANDERMEER, JOHN / The Nicaragua Reader: Documents of a Revolution under Fire / $9.95
17446-1	RULFO, JUAN / Pedro Paramo / $3.95
13012-7	SADE, MARQUIS DE / Justine; Philosophy in the Bedroom; Eugenie de Franval; and Other Writings / $14.95
17979-X	SANTINI, ROSEMARIE / The Secret Fire: How Women Live Their Sexual Fantasies / $3.95
62495-5	SCHEFFLER, LINDA / Help Thy Neighbor: How Counseling Works and When It Doesn't / $7.95
62438-6	SCHNEEBAUM, TOBIAS / Keep the River on Your Right / $12.50
62182-4	SELBY, HUBERT, JR. / Last Exit to Brooklyn / $8.95
17948-X	SHAWN, WALLACE, & GREGORY, ANDRE / My Dinner with Andre / $6.95
62496-3	SIEGAL AND SIEGAL / AIDS: The Medical Mystery / $7.95
17887-4	SINGH, KHUSHWANT / Train to Pakistan / $4.50
17797-5	SNOW, EDGAR / Red Star Over China / $11.95
17939-0	SRI NISARGADATA MAHARAJ / Seeds of Consciousness / $9.95
17923-4	STEINER, CLAUDE / Healing Alcoholism / $7.95
17926-9	STEINER, CLAUDE / The Other Side of Power / $8.95
17866-1	STOPPARD, TOM / Jumpers / $6.95
13033-X	STOPPARD, TOM / Rosencrantz and Guildenstern Are Dead / $4.95
17884-X	STOPPARD, TOM / Travesties / $4.95
13019-4	STRYK, LUCIEN, ed. / The Crane's Bill: Zen Poems of China and Japan / $5.95
17230-2	SUZUKI, D.T. / Introduction to Zen Buddhism / $11.95
17224-8	SUZUKI, D.T. / Manual of Zen Buddhism / $9.95
17599-9	THELWELL, MICHAEL / The Harder They Come: A Novel about Jamaica / $7.95
13020-8	TOOLE, JOHN KENNEDY / A Confederacy of Dunces / $6.95
17403-8	TROCCHI, ALEXANDER / Cain's Book / $3.50
62168-9	TUTUOLA, AMOS / The Palm-Wine Drunkard / $4.50
62189-1	UNGERER, TOMI / Far Out Isn't Far Enough (Illus.) / $12.95
17560-3	VITHOULKAS, GEORGE / The Science of Homeopathy / $12.50

13021-6   WALEY, ARTHUR / The Book of Songs / $8.95
17211-6   WALEY, ARTHUR / Monkey / $8.95
17207-8   WALEY, ARTHUR / The Way and Its Power: A Study of the Tao
          Te Ching and Its Place in Chinese Thought / $9.95
17418-6   WATTS, ALAN W. / The Spirit of Zen / $6.95
62031-3   WORTH, KATHERINE / Oscar Wilde / $8.95
17739-8   WYCKOFF, HOGIE / Solving Problems Together / $7.95

GROVE PRESS, INC., 920 Broadway, New York, N.Y. 10010